Whatever Happened to Antara

And Other Syrian Stories

Modern Middle East
Literatures in Translation Series

Whatever Happened to Antara
And Other Syrian Stories

Walid Ikhlassi

Translated from the Arabic
by Asmahan Sallah and Chris Ellery

Center for Middle Eastern Studies
The University of Texas at Austin

Library of Congress Catalogue Card Number: 2004105607

ISBN: 978-0-292-70282-0

Printed in the United States of America

Cover design: Diane Watts

Series Editor: Annes McCann-Baker

Originally published as *Ma hadatha li'antara,* Manshourat wazaret athaqafa
fi ajumhuriyya al'rabiyya assuiryya, Damascus: 1992.

Partial funding for this publication awarded by the
National Endowment for the Arts

Contents

Contents

Translators' Acknowledgments

First, we acknowledge God for His many blessings and for making possible all the events that had to happen for this translation to be published. Second, we thank Walid Ikhlassi, for very courageously agreeing to give us the chance to translate his book, for spending time with us, and, of course, for writing such a superb book in the first place.

We are deeply grateful to the Center for Middle Eastern Studies at the University of Texas at Austin for making this and other important Arabic works available in English translation. Special thanks to Annes McCann-Baker for recognizing the merit in the project and for her patience and guidance in working with us. We are also grateful to Diane Watts, the artist for the Center, who designed the cover that lets us walk again in the Old City of Aleppo.

To Elizabeth Fernea, our distinguished editor, we offer especially warm thanks for her labor of love on the project and for her insight into the book as expressed in both her astute editing and her excellent introduction.

This project would not have been possible without a Faculty Development and Enrichment Grant from Angelo State University. We are grateful to Don Coers, ASU Provost and VP for Academic Affairs, for approving and funding the project, and to Jim Holland and Jim Moore, our dean and department head, respectively, for their ongoing encouragement and support.

We express our profound gratitude to the J. William Fulbright Scholar Program and the Council for the International Exchange of Scholars. Without that Fulbright, the perfect collaboration would never have been possible. Our special thanks to Gary Garrison at CIES; he provided the nudge at just the right time. And a very loving "Shukran!" goes to Juliet Wurr, Jessica Davies, Sahar Hassibi, and everyone at the American Cultural Center in Damascus.

Introduction

The distinguished writer Walid Ikhlassi is an eloquent spokesperson for the citizens of a new nation. For Syria is literally a new nation. The present independence and government date from 1946, though the area traces its roots into antiquity. Known for millennia as "Syria" and "the Levant," Syria was part of the Fertile Crescent in ancient times, that swath of fertile land that allowed many peoples to live and prosper. It also attracted outsiders. Interested in its resources, Hittites, Babylonians, Assyrians, Egyptians, and Persians ruled for shorter or longer periods, as did the Roman Empire under Pompey. The rise of Christianity was also important in Syrian history; St. Paul after all was converted on the road to Damascus, the present-day capital. The Arabs arrived in the sixth century of the Christian era, and, though many residents converted to Islam, groups of Christians and Jews persisted. After invasions by Mamluks and Mongols, Syria and the Levant finally achieved a measure of self-rule under the Ottoman Empire, beginning in 1516 and continuing until the Empire finally collapsed during World War I. In 1919 and 1920, the victorious allies, Britain, France, and Italy, divided up the Middle East, carving out nation states from the Old Ottoman territories and placing them under what was termed "mandate" supervision. Britain took on Iraq, Aden, the Sudan, and Egypt; Italy got Libya; and Syria was assigned to French governance, along with Algeria, Tunisia, Morocco, and Lebanon. Movements for independence from these colonial-mandate governments began early and led to success in the 1940s and 1950s. In 1946, when all foreign troops withdrew, Syria was declared an independent nation. The past half-century has witnessed more or less successful efforts on the part of the new leaders to redistribute land more equably, upgrade education and health care, and move toward representative government. A 1958 attempt to create, in coalition with Egypt, the United Arab Republic was short-lived. A complex history.

Walid Ikhlassi is a product of this complex history. The author, whose stories we are fortunate to be able to read here in English, is an activist member of his country's parliament, a politician as well as a writer, who takes his civic as well as his artistic responsibilities seriously. When asked which writers have influenced his prolific works of art, short stories, novels, award-winning drama, he cites Anton Chekhov. Chekhov, he has said, inspired him to look at the world and at his nation through ordinary people and in the everyday activities of their lives. He also credits the *Arabian Nights* as an influence, and the oral storytellers of his society, like his own maternal grandmothers.

Thus, the majority of the characters in the stories which follow are men, women, and children with the modest concerns of people in all parts of the world: family, work, health, the turning of the seasons. Trees, flowers, houses, and public buildings also figure in the works, just as they figure in the lives of the characters: "A Walnut Tree for This Time" serves almost as a symbol for the young man trying to come to terms with his ninety-year-old grandfather's determination to take a new wife. In "Lost Ornamentation," the protagonist returns to his home town after years of forced exile and bemoans the decline and deliberate defacing of the once nobly ornamented building, which served as the headquarters for the city's first elected council. And even a lowly insect, crawling slowly across a manuscript, gives the central character hope for the future in "The Worm."

Ikhlassi sets his stories in the neighborhoods where people struggle for a decent living, try to raise their children, and occasionally achieve a sense of community. The values of the neighborhoods and their inhabitants, which emerge from the works, are personal integrity, hard work, and devotion. Excess is frowned upon—an excess of anything, even beauty. The lovely girl Shitaa, center of "My Absent Cousin," is judged to be too much, too attractive for the neighborhood and family into which she is born. And so she leaves—for the promised land known as America.

To an English-reading audience, the stories presented here appear modest, understated. The works in Part One are set in the pre-independence period, when protests and demonstrations were in progress everywhere against the French presence. But the French soldiers do not hold center stage in any of the stories; they appear only through their effects on local people. There is almost no clashing of arms, little dense plotting against the foreign presence, few fireworks, no martial music. Part Two is set in the post-independence period, and again there is no martial music and no fireworks. Instead, Ikhlassi offers subtly told tales of men and women caught in bureaucratic snafus, economic disasters, local corruption, and local political conflicts. The author uses many different narrative strategies to achieve his ends: monologue, flashback, and an artful juxtaposition of past and present, of dream and reality.

However, the title story, "Whatever Happened to Antara," is somewhat different. Antara is a folk hero of Muslim history. Son of an Arab man and a black slave woman, Antara bore the stigma of lowly origins, but through his bravery, wisdom and poetic genius, rose to a position of dignity and power as chief of his tribe. The central character in Ikhlassi's story, named Antar, seems to follow this traditional pattern. He, too, is a boy of dubious origin—his mother is a maid in a public hotel, his father is rumored to be one of the Senegalese soldiers who help the French control Syria. A neighborhood bully, he is reviled and feared by children and adults alike. Yet, in a fierce street battle with armed French police (the only such encounter in the entire collection of stories), Antar charges ahead while others run, and he dies a martyr to the cause of Syrian freedom.

Critics have suggested that for Ikhlassi, Antara (Antar) may represent Syria in both periods, courageous and self-sacrificing during the long struggle against the French, bullying and repressive in the early years of independent nationhood. But, of course, the figure can be read in both ways, and this, I believe, is a reflection of Ikhlassi's achievement. The Syrian audience can appreciate the multiple layers of his Antar tale; the western reader, often ignorant not only of Antara's mythic dimension, but of Syria's history generally, can appreciate its present day relevance: a neighborhood bad guy redeems himself by sacrificing for a larger purpose.

Indeed, most of the stories in the collection might be read in this layered way. The style varies as the narrative conventions shift. The characters' struggles range from disappointment in love to forced exile on grounds of political agitation. But the layered message remains more or less constant: men, women, and children in Syria today survive and maintain their integrity against difficult odds—this is clear to all readers. Methods of survival also vary in the stories: some people immigrate to distant lands such as America, some accept their unhappy marriages, many remain in economic need. What eases such pain and grief? Ikhlassi might answer "poetry." The characters in many stories turn to writing. The husband in "The Worm," who is about to be evicted from the family house, finds solace in the poetry of Mahmoud Darwish. The young, disappointed lover in "My Distant Cousin" inscribes the poetry of his passion on the walls of the local café. The benevolent, wronged father in "My Brother Omar" takes refuge in figures from Islamic history, particularly Omar bin al Khattab, who stand for justice and honor, sentiments which the father tells his wife and children are the finest expressions of humanity. The exiled politician in "Lost Ornamentation" finds solace in a projected book he realizes that he will write in the future.

The reader comes to care about the characters in the stories, as though they were neighbors or friends. Will the wronged father get his judgeship back in the new independent Syria? How is beautiful Shitaa doing in America? And what of the sorrowing city council ex-member in his exile? Is his book coming along well? Ikhlassi's gift, for which he might credit his story-telling grandmothers, is to engage his audience and communicate the common humanity found in the lives of these ordinary people faced with extraordinary challenges. Ikhlassi gives both western and eastern readers a real sense of the daily problems and the hopes of the citizens of a nation still defining itself—contemporary Syria.

Elizabeth Warnock Fernea

4

Whatever Happened to Antara

Part One

A Walnut Tree for This Time

My grandfather angrily stomped his boot on the old flagstones. His boots had not been replaced since my childhood, although their leather was cracked. He roared and neighed in a voice that my grandmother had said "would abort a pregnant woman." That afternoon, he seemed to be regaining his youth. He walked two steps toward me, then stopped to gaze at the row of henna trees, about which his third wife used to say, "Their smell arouses his appetite to sleep with women." He then threw out his chest and shouted, "He who opposes my marriage, let him say it openly, without fear."

Again he gave the floor another blow from his foot; something seemed to be boiling up inside him.

The secret meeting of his sons, grandsons, and sons-in-law was noisy, and the opinions expressed numbered over sixty, the approximate number of those who attended the meeting held in the family's largest house, that of the oldest of the grandsons. Although many of the men did not show up, the meeting was considered legitimate. The only thing I did not expect came at the end, when all of them unanimously agreed to give me the most difficult task. I tried to decline but failed. The determination of the males of the family was something that could be neither ignored nor disobeyed.

The news of my grandfather's desire to get married had gone around the neighborhood through the gossip of old women. They were like bees humming about this man who was ninety years old or more but still desired women. My assigned task was to persuade my grandfather to give up the marriage, which was considered lustful and improper both for him and for the reputation of the family. I cursed that democracy to which the family meeting adhered and to which I was sacrificed. When I tried to excuse myself from the responsibility, one of the uncles rose and made a short embellished speech in which he praised my knowledge and persuasive ability. This, he argued, qualified me to deal with strong men

7

like my grandfather, whom none dared to disobey or argue with on any subject. So I found myself obligated, confused, and searching for a proper way to convey the family's peaceful rebellion to my grandfather, who was not used to accepting contradictory remarks from anyone.

I entered Grandfather's house from the long, dark lane that led to the gate. My heart and my mind raced; I found myself shivering. The wooden gate was open. Its nails still held it together, nails the shapes of which I had liked since I was a child. I felt small in that vast opening. My steps slowed. Grandfather was in the front of the house; he sat cross-legged on one of two chairs used in wedding parties of the family men, for many years. Although I was waiting for my turn to sit on that wedding chair, I could not articulate my wish because I was still studying at the university. My beloved knew about these two chairs and she would sigh. Our love was secret and wishful. Nothing would expose it except perhaps too much meditative staring at the twin chairs of happiness.

Grandfather sat gazing at the marble flagstones. I realized that some decisive ideas might be going around in his head. His voice reached me as if he sensed in my footsteps foreboding and confusion. Thus he murmured, "Come closer. You must be the son of the late Abdullah. God have mercy on you, Abdullah."

I approached him with quicker steps, but he refused to let me kiss his hand as everybody does and said, "You are the most educated among them. Do not kiss anybody's hand."

I muttered shyly, "You are my grandfather."

He laughed and stroked me gently with his index finger: "Say, rather, I am your friend." Inviting me to sit on the other chair, he continued: "I am pleased to have a friend like you, befriended by books. Books arouse one's appetite for living."

I tried to steal a look at his face, which seemed to me during those moments to be as beautiful and solid as the entrance of the Citadel, which he told us he had defended in his youth. Death had fluttered around the fighters, he said, but he had not surrendered. He then said with a profound sigh, "The Citadel and I never grow old."

Suddenly I wished that I had embraced him or that he had embraced me with his long arms. I was thinking of my sweeping love for him. I had never won a single kiss from him, though. On the day of the *Eid*, the feast, we grandchildren used to line up in front of him, and he would survey us like a victorious leader contemplating the readiness of his soldiers in uniform. He would tell a boy to fasten his shoelace and a girl to comb her hair again; he would gently stroke the nose of one child and pinch the cheek of another. We would stand there, completely silent until he had finished distributing the *Eid* pocket money on the palms of our hands, opened up like hope. Then the disciplined withdrawal would begin; we would proceed quietly to the entrance of the big house, and then our noisy cries would erupt in the lane.

Grandfather would never fail to recognize each child. Here is the son of so-and-so. That girl's face has the signs of her mother's intelligence. Meanwhile we would look solemnly at him, his love reaching us silently. Like some leader of a squadron, he was miserly of encouraging words with his soldiers; nevertheless, he gave us the feeling that we were the most precious things he had.

Now, as I waited some moments that he spent meditatively looking about the home as if discovering it for the first time, he said, "The hall is very spacious, as you see." I nodded, recalling the old days, and felt the years fluttering like a bird inside of me.

He said with pride tinged with sorrow: "They grow up....and go..."

From my chest came words involuntarily uttered: "You remain, Grandfather."

But then I regained my calmness and said, "And they always come back to you."

He rose suddenly from his seat, covered with a ram's fleece, a fleece that he replaced whenever he took a new wife. On those occasions, he would choose the biggest ram, the fat meat of which was offered to the guests, and put the tanned and wooly hide on his favorite seat. Now he stood up like a young eagle, walking firmly toward the walnut tree, whose dense branches shaded a large area of the pool. He stared at me and lifted his head. His venerable stature was as upright as the old tree. I tried to say something, but stammered, so I kept quiet. Returning slowly to his seat, he said: "The walnut tree is tough and resists time."

9

During those moments I felt that the man wanted to tell me something but preferred only to hint at it. A solid militant in his youth, he had become in his middle and old age the strict judge concerning the important affairs of the family. But he never behaved in an underhanded way. "If I could be like him..." I thought, but I never dared say it aloud, a wish which had obsessed me since adolescence.

The family meeting about the proposed marriage had been tumultuous. It had been the first of its kind ever. The sons and grandsons, together with the sons-in-law, were united to oppose Grandfather. The idea of a ninth wife for the head of the family was unanimously rejected. The woman nominated for the marriage was said to be a thirty-year-old virgin of whose situation my grandfather had heard by coincidence. After visiting the grave of his last wife, he had neighed like a horse. He had personally supervised the decoration of her tombstone. That woman was just as he described when he spoke to her at the graveside, his tears refusing to flow: "Bless you, woman, best likened to good earth."

In that family meeting, substantial evidence of my grandfather's intent to marry had been available, for it was reported that he had said, "If this virgin woman is strong and good at watering trees and taking care of flowers, then it will be fine to have her as my wife."

My grandfather had been fair all his life, had given every new wife and children their full rights, and had never had two wives at the same time, because he believed in the unity of love between man and woman. Yet now fear was rising in everybody's chest lest a woman come and rob him of his mind and money.

Suddenly, returning to his chair, my grandfather took my hand with a strength envied by young men and spoke loudly: "What is your ambition in this life, son?"

I remembered school days. We often had this question in composition homework: "What profession are you going to choose?"

"What are your dreams for the future?"

I almost always failed to write a piece that would satisfy the teachers and often received their reproachful remarks. Now my grandfather's eyes were chasing me, looking for an answer. In spite of my sincere attempts to find reasonable, well-ordered words, I eventually failed to provide a satisfactory reply.

He said in a shrill voice: "I have no ambition but to assert my will for living."

Then he returned to his chair, murmuring quietly without looking at me: "Now, son of the late Abdullah, tell me, what do you want?"

I lost my courage. Apparently I was not worthy of holding the responsibility of expressing the feelings and ideas of the family members. Instead I found myself muttering meekly: "Nothing, Grandfather. I am fine, thanks to God. I am pleased to sit with you, to see you, to listen to you, and to learn."

From within the folds of the shawl which girdled his wrapped waist, he took out a big iron key, offered it to me, and said, laughing, "Bend the key if you can."

I grabbed the heavy iron key and remembered that it was for the big door that had not been used for decades, for it had always been opened for us.

"Bend the key if you can." I did not try. He took it away from me, saying, "You, all my sons, tell me, how many wars have your generations lost?"

Then, using his emaciated hands, he bent the key with a snapping sound. This made me keep silent, and I offered no comment, neither spoken nor signed. I felt completely helpless.

Moments later, Grandfather stood up and walked again towards the walnut tree. He looked up at its branches, gazed thoughtfully at its fruit, which decorated it like green stars, and said loudly: "I always hear you men, so proud of your ideas, saying that cities never die no matter what."

He struck the trunk of the tree with his fist. Nuts fell, and the sound as they hit the ground was like distant gunfire.

Grandfather said in a deep voice: "Don't you want proof that cities do not die?"

He shook the tree again, and more nuts fell. He continued: "I am just like a city that doesn't die. Am I not genuine proof of that idea?"

He indicated to me to pick up a walnut. I did, and then heard him say softly, "Taste it, my son, it will give you strength."

I chewed the white heart of the nut with a joy shared by my grandfather; the deliciousness of the walnut overcame my intention of speaking about his marriage, the matter I had supposedly come to discuss. Grandfather kept feeding me walnut meat, the taste of which would remain under my teeth for many years. Meanwhile, he smiled at me and didn't say a word.

The Antreek[1]

Nobody knows, in the quarter, the features of which have changed with the passing of years, who brought the word "Antreek" into the common language of the people. Although the local lexicon had been increasing generation after generation, nobody had ever thought of explaining any of the new words. Many years later, one of the cousins, who insisted on going to the Faculty of Arts, would appear and show an interest in strange words and sayings prevalent in his family and in the inhabitants of the old quarters. Then he would say with the confidence of a researcher that my father's grandmother was the one who put this word into the local vocabulary when she cried, so amazed that her heart could have stopped: "The antreek is in the house of Soulaiman Bey."

Soulaiman Bey was one of those eminent people famous for fabulous wealth and known to have many hobbies, such as possessing horses and beautiful women. He married a woman from our family. The woman was a copy of her Albanian white-skinned, large-hipped grandmother, so she was the talk of the town in the old days.

It all started when my grandmother went to visit in the big house that Soulaiman had inherited from his father. The house was divided into four distinct parts, each holding one wife, usually a new woman. The second wife of the husband of my grandmother's cousin had given birth to a boy, so she offered as a present an artificial cluster of grapes, the leaves of which were woven of silver threads. It was her duty, as one of Soulaiman's relatives, to express her joy for the coming of a new heir for the man's glory. Grandmother came to the house in the early evening, and she saw women chanting with their trilling sounds of joy on the occasion. A big lamp hung from the ceiling of the large hall. It was so big and

---

[1] A corruption of the French word *electrique*, meaning electric power.

bright she thought the sun had been tied there by a thread, and she cried out in fright, "What is that strange light!"

The "antreek," they told her, so when she returned home, hallucinating, she was repeating the word "antreek," which nobody understood until later.

Grandmother, who exceeded sixty, though her exact age was unknown, was still in the prime of her strength. Every day she kneaded the dough as if it were a silky head cover and baked it on the *tannur*, the old baking oven, and prepared the bread for at least twenty people in addition to guests and beggars who usually knock at doors during feasts and on cold nights. She would not let anybody draw the water out of the well for her to use for ablution or for washing the huge pots for cooking sheep. She used to pick the leaves of the grapevines herself and keep them in salty water for winter days. She loved the moon and told stories to the little ones, who were fond of her skillfully-woven tales. They listened keenly to pithy proverbs she offered for every occasion. She used symbols in telling stories and told the children that the moonlight did not hurt eyes if the heart was capable of receiving it. One would remember such statements when talking about the "antreek."

When Grandmother's feelings cooled down after the shock she received in Soulaiman Bey's house, she started talking about the electrical lamp in a very cautious way, which is how she behaves when confronted with anything new. One of her granddaughters, who had inherited her honey-colored eyes from Grandmother, with a sigh asked, "Does it look like the moon?"

Grandmother flew out of her chair in the little room and shouted violently, "The antreek blinds one's eyesight, but moonlight wipes away the heart's sadness."

Grandmother did not know how to read and write, but it was known in the quarter that she could read the short verses from the Holy Qur'an, depending on the rhythm of the reciter. She would get lost if the reciter did not excel. Therefore, people said that her speech, which tended toward Standard Arabic while talking about nature, the city, and good people, stemmed from the clarity of soul known only by the pious.

When she talked about the "antreek" for the first time, her words seemed like meteors falling on the heads of her listeners, who gazed at her with alarmed eyes, unable to find an explanation for the babbling of this strong woman, who had never stammered in her life, not even for one day. The words flying from her cold lips seemed to cause, though her mouth had never lost a tooth, a shrill buzzing that filled the people with suspicion. Her family speculated a lot about her case, which pushed the three sisters of my grandfather, who were spinsters famous in town during war and famine, to burn the house's stock of Indian incense that had been saved for calamities. They began muttering feverishly like those who gathered in circles to intensely remember and adore God, "Oh, God, save our sister-in-law from insanity. Oh, God, we do not have the strength to endure the madness of the mistress of the house."

In spite of the historic hate arising between a married woman and her husband's cousins, the sisters' need of Grandmother, who was kind to them out of love for her good husband, made them start the prayer of the *Wadudiah*[2] for seven consecutive days. The house turned into a beehive, and the word *Wadud* flew in the air with a buzzing that numbed both ear and tongue. For many nights, my grandmother watched the "gas toy" sweeping away the darkness from the room among the high walls within which she secluded herself. There, she grumbled slowly as if recalling something lost, "Antreek...antreek..."

Nobody, not even my father himself, knew whether she dreaded that word or longed for it. A few years later, something would happen and guarantee the confusion of those who heard her repeating that word, so they wouldn't know the real meaning of my grandmother's feelings towards that which was called "antreek."

The visit to Soulaiman Bey's house was never repeated. The man, who was over seventy though nobody would give him more than fifty, divorced our cousin because she did not beget boys like his other women (he had also divorced them because signs of aging appeared on their bodies sooner than he expected). The poor woman was returned to her house with a post-marriage dowry of gold, though that did not prevent rejoicing at her misfortune. My

[2]A prayer in which the good name of God, *Wadud,* meaning "the loving," is repeated again and again, sometimes more than a thousand times.

grandmother said at the time, "The antreek blinds both eyesight and perception. God has blinded the man's understanding, so he broke the girl's heart."

So we had no other chance to see in the oft-married man's house the electric lamp, the "antreek," which had changed, people said, into a copper lantern with seven lamps competing with sunlight.

In spite of the fact that electrical poles began to spread along the main street leading to the governor's house, my grandmother never went out at night. So she never saw dozens of the lamps hanging like stars from the sky above the street, a spectacle for people and a miracle for village country folk who asked their mayors to tell them strange stories about the antreek when they came home.

My grandmother continued to associate disasters with electricity. For after the divorce of our cousin, my grandfather spoke openly of his wish to have electricity in the house before his death. However, he also expressed distress because he could not afford it. The widespread increase in prices kept that wish from him, a man who had to provide food for a tribe of mouths. When my grandfather died suddenly after falling off his mule while coming back from the market, my grandmother said, "I wish he had not wanted to get the 'damned' thing into the house."

She remained indignant at that strange novelty of the "antreek" until the accident took place.

Earlier, my grandfather had told his companions at the café, where people gathered around the storyteller, that the antreek would enable them to see the features of the man who recited to them all the stories of the heroes. The café owner had looked at him suspiciously and wondered about that "strange tale" of my grandfather. It was then my grandfather decided to dream of getting electricity into the house, so that he could read the Holy Qur'an better and understand what had been closed to him.

Then came the fatal night of the accident. One of the neighbors, who had married his daughter to an important merchant whose son-in-law was a man in authority close to the governer, boasted to the people of the quarter that he could put an electrical pole in front of his house by himself; he accomplished it in less than two days. The wooden post, painted with asphalt, stood in front of the man's door.

And on the next night, the big lamp spread a wide circle of light on the flagstones of the dark lane. It seemed to give the house a special dignity and respect.

My grandmother heard what happened and in a panic went to the lane to check the news herself. Her eyes fastened on the lamp as doubt painted tension on her face. She trembled and gazed at the strange light, which had dispelled the darkness of the quarter. Suddenly, she shouted in pain as if an arrow had pierced her pupil. From that moment, Grandmother could see nothing but pale shadows, which she said would pass before her.

People said that black water had struck her eyes, and there was no hope that she would ever see again.

Until her last days, my grandmother remained silent, never saying a word about electric lamps, as if she concealed feelings for them which it was not yet time to express. And, in spite of all the spells hung around her neck, my grandmother remained blind.

Afterwards, electricity sneaked into the lane and even into the large house itself, but my grandmother seemed not to sense it except on some evenings. Those were the times when joy entered through the songs and the dancing feet of young men and women. The young people went around and around under the light of the lamp hung from the grape trellis. For it was said that the grapes ripened faster under the heat of the electricity and its light.

My Aunt's Dreams

My aunt claimed that the governor of Aleppo, who lived in the castle with his four women and subordinates, had personally asked her father for her hand in marriage, but she had declined his proposal in spite of the appeals of her family, who met in the main sitting room, thanking God for the favor He had blessed them with. One of the uncles had said, "Our daughter will live in the Citadel. By God, this is a real honor."

An old man who had lost a leg in the Balkan Wars had shouted jubilantly, "Who will help me to get to you in the Citadel?"

But my aunt, who was famous for her strength at a time when women were helpless, had maintained her stubbornness and refusal, which left no traces of sternness on her beautiful face. As my aunt—actually my father's aunt—had said, an honest girl should not cause a man to divorce a woman. That is what would have happened if she had accepted Aleppo's governor as her husband. Aleppo's governor was neither ugly nor hunchbacked nor fat as a barrel, as were most of his men who surrounded him wherever he settled, moved, or stayed at his big palace. However, he was neither young nor handsome enough to tempt young women with his masculinity. But it was said that his voice, which had resounded loudly one day, even once in the Big Mosque, had an irresistible charm.

A dangerous sedition was brewing, so the governor had raised his shrill voice that day as if waving a sword, and the fire was out. My aunt had been infatuated with the strong voice, which had been frequently described by the family men. She said that a man with such a captivating voice could be her husband. But still, even the charm of his voice had not convinced my aunt to marry the governor. As a result, he took revenge against her family, in order to preserve his dignity. He became resentful against them all, and thus many of the members of the family emigrated and died in foreign lands.

After years of listening to her tales and to stories of her beauty about which one could never tire, I reached the age of youth and lust. I started thinking obsessively about our new neighbor, a young woman who had been recently brought as a wife to the house next door, a house belonging to the grim-looking man who never warmly greeted any of the people of the quarter. These people thought that he enjoyed a special status, which allowed him to hurt anyone he wished, so they avoided him. His name became "Father Grimly." I was destined to fall in love with Grimly's wife.

I thought a lot about that young woman who darkened her eyelids with kohl, making them the most beautiful eyes in the quarter. People said in private that the stranger's beauty deprived all the other ladies of any advantage. I thought that this woman with the beautiful eyes was favoring me with meaningful looks, so my heart quivered. I avoided mentioning her in front of anybody lest my lovesick state be exposed. The neighbor wife had become the center of my dreams. It seemed to me that the distracted speech of my aunt had been hinting about this beautiful woman, even though my aunt had not seen her. My aunt could still distinguish light and shadow and the movements of people in her room, which she never left. She said, "The most beautiful thing in a woman, son, is her look."

I said to myself, "What a clever aunt! She reads the ardor in one's heart." When she said, "Love manifests itself first in the eyes," I murmured, "What a wonderful old woman she is; she knows what is hidden."

My aunt was more than ninety years old and found it difficult to move about. So she sat still on an old wooden couch, its sticky cotton mattress had lost its flexibility and therefore could not acquire the shape of the person who sat on it. And the imprint of the successive generations of that family was no longer clear on that couch, even though it had often been used during the first nights of marriages. It looked actually as if it were made for two people to sit on close to each other, exchanging wedding sweets and shy kisses. My aunt, who had witnessed all those weddings, was destined in the end to have exclusive possession of the couch; she boasted that she had never been wedded to any man. She always said that men take more than they give. I used to look at her wildly roaming eyes, and the traces of her past beauty soon led me to think of the neighbor wife, who made me know on calm nights the meaning of insomnia.

When I heard my aunt murmuring poetry verses, unable to distinguish the standard language from the colloquial, I knew that she was either talking about some love, or telling the birds to take an unwanted passion to the unknown areas of the sky, or scoffing at the fate that has denied her eyesight, movement, and love. I tried to understand what she said, but she never recited the same verses twice. She loved me, I think, because I always listened to her with complete respect and attention. I even knew when she drank the hot *Sarm Aldik*, a medicinal plant, to which she had become addicted long ago. Sarm Aldik was a diuretic used against an illness that she feared, an illness that had caused the death of many family members either abroad or on the sick bed in our large house, which was destroyed not long ago by the municipality to build the new slaughter house. To this day, I do not know why Aunt hated all dishes containing meat. Did it stem from the existence of the slaughterhouse close to the house where she lived or did she not find meat tasty and hence became a vegetarian. Actually, she did not eat any food unless she needed it, something that happened once a day. She was losing the acuteness of her hearing, and this gave me the chance to tell her in a low voice about my tortured heart, my silent love for the neighbor. The woman did not appear pregnant, even though a year had passed since her arrival to the quarter in an unprecedented wedding procession.

My aunt would nod her head, as if approving every sentence I murmured or spoke out, blessing my incomparable love. I would say to her, "I see her on the pillow." I would say to her, "I feel her heat with gulps of tea." And I would shout, "I love her, I love her!" And I would say to myself, "She needed a young man like me, not one like the odious neighbor, who can hardly get out from behind the steering wheel of his car because of his laziness, fat, and greed."

My aunt never stopped mentioning Aleppo's governor in her conversations, conversations punctuated by periods of silence which might last for days or follow one another as quickly as death follows life. Although the governor was not the only man in the city who proposed to her, she kept talking of him with especially winning enthusiasm, arousing crazy longing in my heart, compelling me to the window to peep at the neighbor. I would stand behind the curtain, holding its thick fabric, with its torn edges. I felt as though the fabric was impeding my breath, which rose and fell like someone in pain, as I followed the movements of the beautiful one, as she moved to the balcony or went into an inner room, where the windows were opened and moved with the rhythms of her body, and seemed to infuse her dress with inviting desire.

The owner of the soap works, which exports laurel soap to all Muslim countries, had also proposed to my aunt. He had come to the house with two mules, the second one laden with copper pots filled with silk, silver, sugar, burghul, and white flour. Though that proposal came during a period of famine, my aunt had still refused him. She had said then that she could not be a second wife and thus hurt another woman. The current wife of the owner of the soap works, who was a good person, did not deserve to be heartbroken. My aunt did not mention her own beauty, though I knew she had been the most beautiful woman in the city. When I watched our neighbor hanging out clothes to dry, I saw in her my aunt's youth. She moved on the balcony like a butterfly. I imagined that those arms, waving like flags on the day of the Prophet's birthday celebration, were giving me meaningful signs. I would sweat and find no refuge but my aunt's lap. Her bony fingers would run through my hair so I would fall asleep as sadly as a kid who has lost his best toys. I did not have any toys in my childhood apart from the ones my mother had made from scraps of cloth, but my sadness was heartbreaking.

The neighbor's wife was my first love. Before that, I had never known of a woman who could send the fragrance of her juicy body through the space of the lane as sweetly as hers reached me from the facing balcony. I never felt such sweetness at the university when I looked at the female students, carefully searching for intimacy in one of their faces. I had never had a girlfriend, for my shyness was overwhelming; I would look down when I slunk into the lecture room, and this was not often, because I had to work with my mother's uncle in the market in order to help provide for our family. In spite of the fact that my deceased father had taught me to respect the neighbors and what they held sacred, my heart beat for the new neighbor whenever the wind fiddled with her clothing and she would hold it tightly to her youthful body with a shyness that would drive you mad. She would stare at our home with a sweet look of panic and run inside.

I told my aunt I loved someone on whom I had no claim. I fell down at the feet of my aunt, who could not hear the torment of my lovesickness, but still wiped my head with one hand while tapping the side of the couch with her other hand in a nervous gesture that she had always suffered ever since she had come to our house. I remembered my father in his last days sitting silently on the couch where my aunt sat now. His own wicker chair had witnessed those days when he had sat with the secret visitors who had gathered in a circle while my father spoke strongly about freedom and about the strangers who occupied our country. The tales of those days were still living in that house, a legend folded back in time. My aunt said, tapping the leg of the old chair with its blackened wood, "I would not have accepted a stranger's proposal."

Moments later, she touched my face with her fingers, and their cracked skin aroused my longing for the softness of the neighbor's wife.

"How old are you, son?" she asked.

I did not utter a word. She went on murmuring and staring at my face as if she were reshaping it in her imagination.

"You look like your deceased father," she finally said. Then she continued, "He was a man."

I always told myself that my father had died heartbroken. All his life he resisted and fought the nation's enemies, but after independence nobody said a soft word to him. So he had wiped his rifle carefully, wrapped it in our flag, and stowed it in the trunk of his mother, who had died of the yellow epidemic when she was still young.

I wondered whether I would die of sorrow because the one I loved would never hear a single word of love from me. Those words filled my mouth like grief, then changed into a sigh, which nobody heard but Aunt. And Aunt must have thought that I was reciting prayers for the soul of the dead and that I would soon start reciting *Yasin*, the chapter in the holy Quran we used to listen to when we bid farewell to the dead of the family when they died, one after another.

Another marriage proposal came for my aunt from a stranger, who had come for a visit with the chief of the quarter and seven of its eminent people. He had told my aunt's father that, if she would marry him, she would live in his place in the mountains with one hundred servants. The farms, which opened onto the steppe with its livestock and resources, would be at the service of his bride.

My aunt said, about this man, "Well, I saw the stranger from behind the vineyard. He came into the house victoriously, as if the open hall of the house were not spacious enough for his pride. He was fifty years old, his prestige preceded him. I was not thirty yet, juicy as an orange."

The men of the family had asked about the stranger's origins. An old man had said that he was the Sultan's executioner and had amassed a fortune from the falling heads. My aunt had grumbled, "A stranger to the quarter, the city, and a stranger to the people I love. How could I accept him?"

The beautiful neighbor woman gradually became part of the quarter; for me she became the quarter itself. Although she had come as a stranger, she had become now closer to my heart than a rush of blood. When the news was passed around to the women that the stranger had not yet become pregnant, although more than a year had passed, it was said also that no plant could thrive except in its own land. I felt that a point in my favor had been scored. I did not allow my fantasies to follow the women of the quarter when they tried to describe her in her marriage bed sharing with that elephant the feverish feelings of love. I murmured to the face of my aunt, who had surrendered to a nap of satisfaction, "Yes, I am sure that she exchanges my feelings of love."

And I thought that, if things went right, my dreams would come true.

One day I asked my aunt whether she had ever loved anyone. She did not answer. Rather, her eyes fixed themselves on empty space. I told myself she had not heard me, so I asked again whether she had ever loved someone with whom fate did not unite her, thus making her love even stronger. Her eyelids twitched as if saying she did not understand the question, so I repeated it more intensely. A muscle near her mouth quivered, then her face regained its stillness. I said to myself, "Is there any hope that love is destined to live?"

I begged my aunt to comment on a letter I had written, filled with longing, which I read to her, but on that day she seemed to me as though she never heard a word or that she ignored all my loving words about the neighbor. She sat still on the couch as if announcing her intent to remain silent, which indeed she did for long days. The letter, which I had not yet tried to send to the beloved, had shaken me as I read it to my aunt as if I were listening to its words for the first time. I simply folded it and settled it close to my heart, and I resumed watching from the curtain and waiting for the beautiful one to appear.

I did not know despair; standing did not tire me, even through many hours and days. I had hopes that she would appear on the balcony and stare at our house out of the corners of her eyes. Then I heard by chance that Grimly had divorced his beautiful, barren wife and returned her to her parents. I was so dismayed that my face in the mirror looked like that of a man whose worries had creased his eyes. Soon, however, I started to listen to my aunt's quiet breaths. Full of satisfaction, I told myself that what had happened was the best chance for me to obtain the love I longed for. I dared not inquire about the beautiful one's new address. I thought I would inevitably come across her either on a street or in a park. I would run to her with all the yearning I had for her and tell her, "I wrote to you, you did not answer." She would reply that the letter did not reach her, and I would remember that the paper was still close to my heart. I would blame myself, and she would pity me and announce that she would be angry with me if I did anything to hurt myself. I would say, "I love you." And she would say, "I love you." We would utter in one voice, the words flying high in space, which belonged to us, murmurs that no one would understand but those who knew love.

One evening my aunt said, "You reached the age of manhood long ago. Your days at the university are about to finish. Aren't you going to look for a good wife?" She went on grumbling some words, something to do with the head of the merchants at the City Market. He had also proposed to her, but she had refused him because she did not want to disturb his daughters. I was wondering at that moment when I could face the beloved and still restrain myself, which I needed to be able to do in a difficult situation like meeting her for the first time.

I asked myself, "Will the years of waiting last long?"

The Elephant Ear

My little aunt was stricken with a big sadness. As a result, she never left her seat in the prestigious part of the western *diwan*, or living room, of the large house that she had refused to leave after marriage for a modern apartment in the new region of the city. Her husband, whom God blessed with a great deal of money from a profitable trade in which he dominated his competition, shared her sadness. In spite of the gloom that filled the house, gray hair did not appear on my forty-year-old aunt's head as it had on her sisters'. She never stopped repeating the same sentence: "I will not leave the place where everything started, no matter what disasters come."

The seat on which she sat was a chair chosen by her grandfather, a man who remained a warrior to his last days. While still a virgin, she had covered the seat with a cloth she embroidered and then lined with taffeta. She sat in the chair and stared at the green plant, the elephant ear, which she loved more than all the other plants in the diwan, on the windowsills, and in the garden. The anxiety that overwhelmed her made her forget to apply her make up, with which she had always taken great pains before. Her husband, who worked hard, had found no comfort but in her beauty; she always met him at the entry of the house as if she were a bride who has just been carried across the threshold. My aunt sat face to face with the elephant ear, watching, moaning, and reciting prayers, resorting for the first time to her grandmother's rosary to recite her appeals to God. It was said that her grandmother would heal incurable disease with her blessed recitations on that rosary. My aunt's grief was terrible in those days.

My aunt's husband tried to understand the situation, and he consulted with his old wet nurse, who still came to the house to manage household affairs. She was a black Ethiopian woman with a face as radiant as a moonlit summer night. Her hair was frozen

27

in small wheels resembling a crown of stiff herbs. The wet nurse said: "A woman without a child is a tree without fruit, and thus feels sad all the time."

At these words, the man became closer to his wife. He was good-hearted and loved my aunt a great deal, and he agreed to live with her at her parents' to avoid his family's gossip and the scolding they gave him for being a "house son-in-law." He announced to his wife as vehemently as he could that he did not like children. My aunt's eyes overflowed with tears and she murmured: "But I want to give you a child. People are jabbering that I'm sterile."

The man shouted back, which was not his habit: "But we were favored once with a child, whom God—with a wisdom we do not doubt—chose to have beside Him."

It was true. A decade before, my aunt was proud of her belly, which became as round as the Chinese jar my aunt's husband bragged about. She would walk in the courtyard and swagger coquettishly. Women said she was going to have a baby girl because she became more beautiful, and that is a sign. The husband bet that the baby would be a boy to whose beauty all the world's gold could not compare. When alone, my aunt wished the baby to be healthy, soundly built, and born painlessly. She lit two candles in the main part of the diwan and would often exchange the melted ones with two fresh ones made from beeswax; she would feed her husband honey every morning so that he would remain the master of men. That is why at fifty plus he enjoyed a level of virile activity envied by the men of the family, both young and old. During the ninth month, my aunt kept an eye on the two lighted candles to keep them glowing, proclaiming in public: "I will not allow evil devils to sneak into the house in the dark."

In the last days of her pregnancy, labor pains started more than once, but she resisted courageously. When she felt that it was her time, she herself called on the same midwife who had delivered her. She lay on her father's small bed, refusing her mother's better copper bed, saying jokingly to her sister and the women of the two families, "My mother gave birth to girls. I want a boy for his sake."

And so it happened. My aunt's husband received the news of the coming of his son with a calm joy. But, when he was told that the child had died, he shouted angrily, refusing at first to believe, but then asking God's forgiveness. Nevertheless, he lost his grip on reality and remained unbalanced for a long time. He neglected to shave; his beard looked like that of a real lunatic completely devoid of reason.

At that time it was said that a curse lay on the house, which had been deserted by all of its people except for my aunt. But such a rumor could not be maintained when the secret became known: the couple's blood was mismatched and this had caused the child to die. Nobody knew whether my aunt's husband had visited doctors and asked for scientific analyses or whether he felt too proud to do that because his own pride was limitless. At any rate, he held on to his belief that his son had been infected by some evil eye because of his extreme beauty, inherited in his family through generations. Had it not been for the great love he had in his heart for my aunt, he would never have agreed to live on in the old house. He would have listened to his family, who appealed to him to marry a woman who could bear many children, thus keeping the family name and its trading business alive.

In the first year after the baby's death, my aunt suffered from the pain of separation. In the next few years, however, the hope of having other children started all over again. She followed the instructions of old women in using amulets, but she was soon occupied by breeding cats and plants. She began to favor plants, because they do not leave the house during mating season. My aunt put together a collection of leaves and flowers that competed with the beauty of the trees growing in her own family home. My aunt's husband used to bring back from his travels exotic seedlings to which the city people were not accustomed. It was said that he was the first to bring a slip of "elephant ear" from a Greek island famous for its charming natural beauty and fertile women.

He used to stand and stare at the large green leaves of the plant and pass his finger gently over the long stem of a high leaf and say: "Noble, proud, upright—just like you, my love."

In the beginning the plant had four leaves. The swollen stem of another soon sprouted, showing the pointed head of a small bud turning around itself slowly as if imitating the circular movement of celestial bodies, following the sunlight for two or three days, after which a whole leaf appeared, grew, and became stronger. A week or more later, it looked like the mother leaf. My aunt announced a new birth and celebrated by distributing almond drink to the neighbors, which is customarily offered in celebrations. My aunt's husband was willing to please her, so he celebrated by offering the meat of a whole sheep to the poor of the neighborhood, who were increasing daily because of the exorbitant food prices, which attacked the city like voracious wild cats during the drought.

The night when the elephant ear sprouted marked the commencement of happiness in the old house. The mood would continue until the new leaf was perfectly grown. Then neighbors and people of the quarter said: "The housewife must be expecting a baby."

A group of singers performed in the evening. The party went on until dawn. None of the relatives and friends who were invited to eat and chat during the night had any clue to the secret of the evening party. My aunt's husband hinted at it, though. He subtly suggested that it had to do with something called "the celebration of the continuation of love." People rejoiced. The high walls of the house echoed the high-pitched songs as if a real wedding were being held. On those evenings, my aunt wore a plain, white gown, ornamented with a ruby on her breast, and she seemed the most beautiful lady the town had ever seen.

Suddenly, the leaves of the elephant ear stopped sprouting. The plant kept its five leaves for a while, but soon the edges of one of them turned yellow, as if burnt. It withered and bent towards earth in such humility that it pained the heart. Neither water nor fertilizers could revive it. When the second leaf withered, my aunt screamed, "Woe is me!" "Be patient," her husband said. "An evil eye must have hit it," she said. When the third leaf died, followed by the fourth, my aunt stood still before the last leaf, praying to God to keep it alive. Greater sadness was yet to come.

The single, remaining leaf seemed still and lonely after the other leaves were cut. My aunt looked at it with horror and hope. After she had tired herself airing the soil and raking it with the end of my grandfather's sword, which was decorated with silver, she resorted once more to the rosary. But the leaf suffered loneliness for a whole month. The swelling of the stem came to nothing.

My aunt said to her husband, "I want my plant to survive."

The death of the last leaf would mean the end of the elephant ear.

That leaf turned yellow, and the sides shriveled and wrinkled. My aunt looked at her hands and, seeing the veins protruding from the skin, became terrified. Silence was heavy everywhere in the house. Even the black wet nurse seemed to share the sadness and seemed willing to die for the sake of love, love that used to fill the house. Her movements became slower. Her hair on the white sheets left traces that frightened my aunt. She became withdrawn, like a person who believes she will lose everything.

Early fall attacked the trees all over town. They surrendered, yielding their leaves one by one. The journey of escorting leaves to their last house seemed endless. My aunt, however, who was preparing herself to lose the elephant ear, decided (while standing one day in front of the stony mirror that the family had passed down through generations) that she would recover her beauty, which had been buried under layers of worry and sorrow. So she colored her eyes with kohl and sprinkled her hair with Arabian jasmine and henna. She asked the wet nurse to burn incense at the west window so that the breeze would carry the smell all over the house, to the bedroom and the copper bed with its silk sheet, sewn by hand and finished by her mother after two generations of women had worked on it. My aunt had imagined that she would present the sheet and the bed to her daughter to enjoy eternal love with her husband. She had taken the sheet out of the closet that day, shaken off the pieces of perfumed soap and laurel leaves, and spread it out on the bright yellow bed. Then she went out into the diwan, as if to look her last on the elephant ear.

My aunt would then continue the story, which she repeated tirelessly for many days afterwards: "I saw the stem of the dead leaf sprouting a little bud."

She had screamed, "God, how could birth come out of death?"

But the new leaf was real and could not be denied. My aunt had touched it very tenderly, her heart quivering at the sight.

My aunt, whose beauty was stunning as never before, would touch her belly gently whenever she recited what had happened to her that day. She would rush to check her dear plant, the elephant ear, and laugh, laughter that buried all the sadness that had ever lived in the house, where many people were born and from which even more would come.

The News of
Sheikha[1] Ibrahim

A few months before independence, my brown-skinned aunt died of a fever in childbirth. She was the youngest girl in the family, so she had been spoiled in her childhood. When she was ten, she still preferred boys' games. The fortuneteller in whom my grandmother trusted said that her being brunette would be lucky and that she would have a long-lasting marriage. But the poor girl died before she turned twenty.

Her husband, Ibrahim Afandi, bewailed her as no man ever before bewailed a wife. He tore his clothes and hit his head against the wall. He shouted incomprehensible words, and his sobbing was louder than the woes of the women who gathered in the courtyard of the small house, lamenting and moving like chickens before laying eggs. The husband's deep grief was merciless in the beginning. This crying mixed with anger, and eventually Ibrahim Afandi fainted. The hunchbacked barber of the quarter had to sprinkle the grief-stricken husband with rose water three times before the burial ceremonies and a fourth time afterwards. The funeral took place on a Thursday, under ceaselessly pouring rain. The old women of the quarter celebrated the death of the bride, for they claimed that her death the day before Friday was evidence of her piety and that she must have been blessed and would go straight to Paradise. Such sayings did not console Ibrahim Afandi, who looked in those days older than his forty-plus years. His eyes remained red for seven days and nights.

The midwife had been the one who announced the news. She had stood at the bottom of the narrow stairs that linked the house courtyard to the diwan and had yelled, "Woe is me! The young

---

[1] The word "Sheikha" in Arabic is the feminine of "Sheikh"—a man respected for his knowledge of religion or else for his age or for his status in the tribe. Ibrahim is a name for males.

woman is gone!" At these words, my grandmother, who had just arrived, collapsed. The husband, Ibrahim Afandi, drew his gun and dashed up the stairs towards Death, wanting to shoot It, but the gun, which he had never used, not once in his life, fell to the floor, and sparks flew out of it. Meanwhile, the tears in his eyes kept this man, who was destroyed by the calamity, from seeing anything but nothingness.

Death had come, disguised at first as a simple fever, which attacked my aunt's exhausted body. It moved through her body for two days and one night after the childbirth, so the poor girl could not even enjoy looking at her first born, who had the sweet features of her beautiful face. Ibrahim Afandi came to stand before his wife's half-closed eyes, seeing the bright drops of sweat covering her face, her lips blue as if Death were taking the young woman away in one decisive blow. The man would shake his wife's shoulder gently, then would ask her, calling her name twice as was his habit in the morning of every day, to hurry and bring him coffee. He would talk to her, pleading, "I am Ibrahim!" He was denying what was happening; he would call her but she would not answer. He would cry out like a beast: "Why? Why?! It can't be, this is unfair!"

One of the female relatives hugged him before he fainted, and she scolded him, saying: "Do not object to God's will, Ibrahim Afandi!"

The man collapsed so completely that they said afterwards it was only God's mercy that brought him back to life after his body seemed to turn into a motionless mass.

Ibrahim Afandi looked more composed on the third day of the funeral ceremony, with which all the quarter was occupied, listening to the blind sheikh reciting verses from the Surat Al Kahf chapter of the Holy Qur'an. He was still working as a private driver for the French security officer in the area, whose arrival caused such turbulence that the men violated the solemnity of the funeral and applauded. That night, Ibrahim Afandi looked more confident of his masculinity; he had shaved, and he shook hands with the other men of the quarter, thanking them for their sympathy. The third day after the death, a rumor was heard in family circles, indicating that my aunt's husband was the real killer of the beautiful brown girl. The gossip suggested the marriage had been a mistake, but such talk was confined within the walls of the house. This was due to fear that Ibraham Afandi might take revenge, for he was now perceived as the strongest man in the quarter after the condolence visit of his French boss accompanied by guards, the Senegalese soldiers who terrified the city. Then the rumor suggested my grandmother was to blame, because she had given up her daughter, even though relatives and strangers warned her that Ibrahim Afandi had a mistress, one of those prostitutes who worked at the brothel. My grandmother started to cry and wail, repeating, "How could I have known?" My grandfather looked at her with silent censure. The mumbled talk turned into a truth which everybody believed: my aunt had gotten childbirth fever because she was deeply hurt by her husband's repeated infidelity, which had been exposed to everyone during the last months of her pregnancy. But that truth was soon to recede and hide itself in the hearts of those who had first believed in it.

My grandfather, on whose face glared light and sadness, stayed silent after losing his daughter; he had always favored her with sweets, which he would stuff into her little mouth. He did not comment on the death apart from piously reiterating, "We submit to God's will. He is the best to trust." He had caused himself trouble once by objecting to the marriage, because Ibrahim Afandi was over forty and the girl was still young. However, his opposition had only sent the house into a flaming rage. My grandmother screamed and repeated sarcastically, "Do you want her to get married to your lunatic poet friend?"

It was true that a young man of the neighborhood had fallen in love with my aunt. He had covered the corners of the quarter and the sides of the café with lines from his poetry celebrating his love for a brunette over whose beauty, he said, the dull old stones of the city would burst into laughter, rejuvenating the youth and vitality of the city. Birds would alight on the boughs of the trees, he wrote, singing to the young woman who passed by with joyfully dancing footsteps.

The poet was poor and was studying religion at the very famous Khoussraywa School in Aleppo. He sent his mother to propose to the girl, but the poor woman returned sadly, as though a knife of derision had stabbed her in the chest, mercilessly done by my grandmother as if into the heart of the young man's love for my aunt. Although my grandfather continued to welcome the young man into his small shop and listened to his poetry with an ecstasy that only a lunatic knows, things went as my grandmother had planned. The poet's heart was broken. The girl married Ibrahim Afandi. She went to the bridegroom's house in a procession accompanied by the brass band of the French army itself. The soldiers of the band were actually from the town and spontaneously played the popular melodies glorifying freedom. They came to the old courtyard of the house, which is overlooked by the Citadel. Its position often worried the occupation army so much that they tried to tear it down with weapons and the blows of shoes, bristling with steel nails and going around the city for the purpose of vigilance and inspection.

Visiting his wife's grave for the third and last time, Ibrahim Afandi was amazed to see flowers scattered on the nearby hill. He picked up one of the stems of henna, stared at it suspiciously, and then threw it away. He tried to separate the remaining stems in order to discover the secret of who laid those flowers there. He said to himself, finally, "It must be one of her folks."

The poet kept inundating the grave with flowers and tears for long years. He became well-known to the gravediggers, who sometimes invited him for a cup of tea. He would sit with them, talk to them about love and the injustice that strikes the living and scars the memories of the dead.

Ibrahim Afandi, who kept his job after the country's independence, married the widow of a local police officer who used the internationally-banned dum-dum bullets to resist the demonstrations held by the people a few days before the independence was declared. As a result, angry people battered the officer with stones, knives and old shoes. The widow came to like Ibrahim Afandi while he was taking care of her deceased husband's compensation papers and paying the postage and other fees from his own pocket. To the widow, he was someone with "a tongue that would call a serpent out of its den," as she described him to her female friends; they congratulated her on her new marriage with words of envy wrapped in the usual hypocrisy.

After that marriage, our family members stopped visiting Ibrahim Afandi's house to look after the dead woman's son. My grandmother said at the time that men couldn't be trusted; she kept cursing the deceased woman's husband and my grandfather, too. The new wife looked after the motherless little child so carefully that she aroused the admiration of everyone, but she stopped when she gave birth to her own first child by Ibrahim Afandi. Her tenderness to the first son stopped as well. My grandmother, who was recently widowed, continued to sneak out to the neighbors and would hug her grandson tightly to her breast. Her eyes would fill with tears, which it was said were the signs of deep regret. But quite soon the grandmother died, and the rest of the family filled the child's ears with talks of his real mother's beauty and suffering. As a result, he grew up sad, signs of depression settling on his brown skin and leaving traces in the pores of his face, almost as if he had been created to bear alone the burden of mourning for that young woman whom both husband and time had betrayed.

The little boy was to grieve even more when his stepmother died of cholera, which swept through the quarters of the poor. For, although she had neglected him in terms of affection, she had fed him well. About that time, Ibrahim Afandi was forced to retire for his own good. He was dismissed for accepting a bribe while mediating between the police administration and well-known smugglers. So he bought an old car and made it a taxi, in which he went around the city earning a living for his children. When the car would break down, he would stop to fix it himself. That car contained parts of most cars in the world—the steering wheel from a Chevrolet, the engine from a Mercedes, and the front doors from an antique Ford carriage. That strange car served as an introduction to his third wife. She had four heavy gold pairs of bracelets, which compensated for her barrenness and brought back grace to her arms. She gave them to her husband, who replaced his strange vehicle with a new car, which attracted many clients, especially from among the nightclub dancers on late nights. They got used to Ibrahim Afandi and his moral bearing, which did not prevent him from peeping at their legs and breasts and heaving sighs as they staggered along drunkenly, a condition with which their exhausting work usually ended. Those miserable women were attracted to Ibrahim Afandi, who gave them pieces of advice mixed with religious sayings of his own invention. As a result, he would reluctantly accept a large fee while hiding an untamable desire to be alone with one of these women in order to prove to her the masculinity still boiling in his veins.

Ibrahim Afandi kicked out his third wife because she annoyed him with her talk about the financial aid, which she had provided him to improve his status from a driver of a "tired mechanical donkey" into an owner of a respectable car. He was able to quash her complaint accusing him of frittering away her money. Her defense—that she had trusted him and so had not asked for a receipt for the gold bracelet—did not result in her recovering her money. Ibrahim Afandi even convinced the judge of his reasons for divorcing her so humanely after putting up grudgingly with her cruelty and maltreatment of his five poor children.

When he was over sixty, Ibrahim Afandi married again, arousing the admiration of the men of the quarter and their gossip, while his round-faced new wife pranced around, returning the visits of the ladies. She was slim and playful with the exuberance of youth. The talk, both in secret and in public, concerned the masculinity of the man, whose tiring day job did not seem to prevent him from performing night duty. The new wife terrified the children with her shrill voice, which clanged loudly through the courtyards as she gave them orders while sitting on the wooden sofa, a sofa that had witnessed past days of happiness. She was fond of smoking the hubble-bubble, a habit she had acquired while working for a family which ran a gambling house. Although Ibrahim Afandi never risked a single piaster at the gambling tables, he was able to persuade that woman to live with him, though not for very long. One day, she disappeared along with all the money the man had been saving for a larger house to hold his increasing family. He had solid connections with policemen, to whom he provided the important service of regularly reporting what people in the quarter were saying, and the passing drivers' slips of the tongue. But this did not help him to get back his runaway wife or recover the stolen money.

Ibrahim Afandi remained depressed after these incidents. His pride was at a low ebb until a woman about fifty years old accepted him as husband. Before that, she had been the wife of the mosque *muezzin*, who had dizzily fallen from a small minaret and been killed instantly. It was said that it was ecstasy that had overwhelmed him when he was singing *al madaa'h an-nabawiya*.[2] He had fallen and died as a martyr to be buried at the mosque wall next to a holy man, whose origin was unknown. The wife resorted to her connections at the Office of Religious Endowment and got Ibrahim Afandi appointed *muezzin*. But his voice never helped him to entice people for the prayers, which he himself had not performed before. So he shared his salary with a poor student, who called the prayers at the five appointed times instead of him. Ibrahim Afandi had to wear a small tarboosh striped with an embroidered band in order to win people's respect. He found the sobriety he assumed to his taste and started sitting for a long time in the empty room annexed to the mosque to relax after his tiring job as a driver, or else to escape the children's problems and their requests. These were numerous and varied, ranging from his eldest son's desire to get married to one of his daughter's insistence on buying a new dress in order to be in the prevalent fashion.

One day, Ibrahim Afandi broke his leg in a collision that totaled his car. He began spending his time in the mosque room, reading old books on magic and the interpretation of dreams. A woman whose milk had gone knocked on his door and asked him to read over those dried-out breasts some blessed words. Ibrahim Afandi was charmed by the buxom chest, which he could see while reciting the blessed words and reading from a book, the pages of which were yellow and worn. When some drops of milk dripped down, filling his palm, the woman chanted joyfully and gave him a lot of money. And so, the news circulated in the quarter that Ibrahim Afandi performed miracles. Since he was dealing mostly with women and sitting on felt for long hours, he felt compelled to wear his wife's cotton dress. Hence, with the passing of time, he came

---

[2] Very moving poems sung in remembrance of the qualities of Prophet Muhammad.

to be called "Sheikha Ibrahim." Troubled young women who had lost their husbands, spinsters whom no one had asked for in marriage, and women who had not been blessed with children all came to trust in him. The eyes of Sheikha Ibrahim glittered behind the magnifying lens that he used to explore the worlds of beauty and charm of the bodies undressing in front of him; he trusted that these women would be able to give love or that they would survive sickness or deprivation. Eventually, Ibrahim Afandi lost the wife who opened to him a career which saved him from the troubles behind the steering wheel and from staying up at night. But he did not marry again. Apparently, he was satisfied by the fact that hundreds of women called him lovingly and respectfully "Sheikha Ibrahim...Sheikha Ibrahim..."

My Absent Cousin

1

My third cousin was born in the dawn of one of the last days of the last month of a severe winter, the like of which the region had not witnessed for half a century. Fuel was scanty and snow abundant, embracing the city as if in love with it, wearing it down out of exhaustion, hunger, and fear. The little cousin was skinny and scarcely filled the hands of the midwife with blessing, as she put it, and it was said that the lungs of the newborn were forcefully opened so the child could breathe. After thinking a long time, her father named her Shitaa (winter), not for the sake of a season whose rain brings welfare, but rather to keep away the evil of any envious person who might ask, "How did this creature survive in times of cold and poverty?"

During family gatherings, Shitaa's news was mentioned whenever the old people talked about bad omens, and finally she became associated with bad luck. My aunt's husband, Shitaa's father, an employee at the mayor's office, was put in jail a year after Shitaa was born. He was freed at the beginning of her fourth year, crippled and unable to walk without crutches; although he was proved innocent, he lost his job, and the security forces were never satisfied with the silence that he maintained. In Shitaa's second year, her only older brother was infected by smallpox; sores ate his face and bit his left eye. When Shitaa turned six, a famine spread through the city due to war and drought. Wheat was hidden in the cellars of merchants and rich people to keep it away from the eyes of the poor. For the first time, I heard an old woman saying: "Some kids are bad omens for their families and countries." Although I was born in the same year as my cousin, I understood that grim-looking old lady's remark did not refer to boys like me. I did not feel proud, however.

Shitaa's thin body bloomed with early femininity, but even her beauty became a curse after a struggle for her hand began. Some men tried to gain favor from Shitaa's father, my aunt's husband, who sat behind the small window of a kiosk where he sold cigarettes, sweets for kids, and newspapers and magazines (which he read himself for entertainment). He never turned down any suitor's proposal to marry Shitaa; instead, he would reply to the suitor in a noncommittal voice, "The good is what God has chosen." The listener would think that this prayer indicated agreement. But it all led to tragedy. The owner of shipping trucks, who had sworn to marry Shitaa no matter the cost, ran over the cosmetics merchant, who was famous for dyeing his white hair with henna and who had sworn by his six children in the market in front of a crowd that he would marry Shitaa even if he had to sacrifice all his fortune for her, whom he called the most beautiful girl in the whole world.

The boss of Bouzing was what the king of trucks liked to call himself, once he dominated the roads in most of the country. By then he had acquired respectability as well as a large truck and trailer. He tried to get rid of the increasing number of suitors for the hand of my cousin, who had not realized yet the importance of her stunning beauty. That beauty was described by the family and the ladies of the quarter as if made by Satan himself; but in fact, her beauty was the kind of gift from God rarely given to any of his creatures. Later, we learned that the boss of Bouzing had made a list of his competitors; not one was less than forty, the age known to be the age of ripeness and masculinity. The big cosmetics merchant topped the list. A truck waited for him at the beginning of the street where he lived and where he returned every day. The moment the man attempted to enter his house, a heavy vehicle rolled forward, leveled his plump body on the asphalt, and then sped crazily away. No one was able to get its number or dared to provide a description of it, so the investigation ended attributing the murder to "a person or persons unknown." Even so, the case was soon known to every one related; the beautiful Shitaa was cited as the cause of a curse which afflicted her family, and it was said she drove men crazy. In the end, the king of trucks seemed to be afraid of carrying out his plans to marry Shitaa; he acted as if he had forgotten his ambition to add the young woman to his household. Eventually, Shitaa disappeared forever from her house and from the quarter. Nothing was left of her but some cloudy memories in the minds of the neighbors, and grief in the heart of the one who truly loved her.

2

Shitaa excelled at school. The principal liked her and favored her but felt uneasy as she noted Shitaa's perfect marks on exams and assignments, for she was afraid that other teachers wanted to share Shitaa's love. Eventually, the spinster principal was unable to separate her sweeping love of Shitaa and her fear of others' opinions, so that love blended with hate, her tenderness with cruelty. Poor Shitaa did not know what to think, especially after one stupid student with blond hair launched a campaign of hate against Shitaa; she spoke of Shitaa's poverty and invented lies about her behavior. Thus Shitaa learned patience as well as astonishment, and would come back home every day as usual. No one could tell whether her face showed sadness or meekness. She would sit next to the doll which an aunt of hers had made for her out of old scraps of cloth. Into the body of the doll the aunt would plunge pins to keep evil and envy away from Shitaa. The doll did not have clear features but apparently could understand Shitaa's silent sadness.

Shitaa became the only daughter of her parents, after her two sisters married and her brother left for distant countries, both to earn a living and to avoid the local eyes, which used to stare at his pock-marked face. Shitaa continued to fill her parents' house with life and goodness. As soon as she finished her homework, she would be preparing food in the kitchen, cleaning the rooms and the courtyard, or else helping her disabled father use his crutches so gently that his eyes would fill with tears and he would pray for her to be protected from wolves. Shitaa would wonder what he meant by the wolves, because she knew nothing about them apart from what she had read in schoolbooks and novels. She had been very fond of books ever since she had learned how to read and write at an early age. Her father would answer ambiguously as usual, as if his

43

prison term had taught him to be cautious in whatever he said or did.

My older brother was a reckless young man who smoked and chased girls in the modern part of the city. He also used to frighten the young men of the quarter with a knife that he had made himself out of the bones of a turkey we devoured on one of the few feasts when our family was happy. He changed suddenly into a hardworking student and decided to study again for the baccalaureate to prepare for the university and a respectable career. He seemed hurt by Shitaa's departure, which we never expected.

3

The first indications of my brother's interest in his cousin appeared when she visited us after a long absence. She was playing with the girls in the courtyard; her small breasts shook under the cotton dress my mother had given her, and her braids flew in the air like the tail of a noble horse. On that day, the Arabian jasmine sprouted, birds gathered on the twigs of the bitter orange tree, and water suddenly poured into the pond that had been sluggish for a long time. For three days and nights, my brother seemed struck dumb. In the darkness, I could hear him tossing and turning on the bed next to mine, repeating in his sleep, "Shitaa...Shitaa..."

I kept the secret, never telling anybody for fear he might beat me up. Besides, at first I was not honest with myself about my own ambiguous attraction towards my cousin. I would fall asleep, and she would appear to me from behind a flowing waterfall, her dress stuck to her rosy body, and seeing me, she would smile and stretch out her hands, and I would run to her, panting. But the dream would end mercilessly, and I would wake up burning with ambiguous desire and paralyzed by the fear that someone might learn of my dream, which did not change throughout my youth.

As for my brother, he shouted once to my mother's face as she was bending over the laundry tubs: "I want to get engaged!"

She was scrubbing a sheet at the time, but replied, "Who wants to get engaged...who wants to get married?"

My brother was ferociously stomping the stones in the court-yard, which were full of holes. He repeated: "That's right. Who wants to get engaged, wants to get married." Then with sudden tenderness, his eyes glancing at the Arabian jasmine, he added, "My cousin."

"Your cousin! Who do you mean?"

"My cousin Shitaa."

My mother shook the soapy water from her hands and then looked at my brother as if she did not understand yet what he meant. With his tall build, which I envied him for, he looked like a horseman or a warrior awaiting a response to his challenge. Suddenly, my mother said loudly: "She is my niece, of my own blood and flesh, but she's a bad omen for her folks, son."

My brother shouted, "I will not tolerate any more bad words about Shitaa." He shouted with a twenty-year-old's violence, an emotion that showed the protruding veins in his neck. The ropes of garlic and drying meat hanging in the courtyard shook at his voice.

Mother resumed washing the laundry, murmuring: "Well, do you love her more than me?"

His bold confessions flew from his lips. I was extremely upset but dared not do anything yet.

"I love her," he shouted, "and I will always love her and I want her and she will never be someone else's and woe to he who stands in my way."

4

In the general exams of the secondary school, Shitaa ranked first of all the students of the city even though she was younger than average. As a result, one of our neighbors, whose son did not pass the exam, whispered wickedly that the girl had passed only because the male and female supervisors of the exams could not resist her charm. And the local newspapers did not publish Shitaa's photo, as was the custom in honor of the best students, because they could not locate her address, which was in a forgotten section of the Old City.

There was no question that she came first in terms of beauty; my brother and I were of the same opinion—publicly on his part, secretly on mine—so we did not allow anybody to say that another's beauty surpassed Shitaa's. However, the girl's great success became a disastrous curse on both the public love (my brother) and the secret one (me).

Shitaa disappeared suddenly. The first to sense her absence was my brother, whose unexpected success in the baccalaureate exams motivated him to visit his aunt's house bravely. He seemed not to care the least for my mother's and the family's warnings, and he challenged every one who thought of wooing her.

On the first visit, he dared not ask about her; rather he kept chatting with my aunt about childhood memories and future ambitions. On the second, he asked whether Shitaa was at home, but he did not get a clear answer. However, the third time, he took a present out of his breast pocket—a small box that he himself had made from bone, for Shitaa to keep within it the precious jewelry and presents that she would receive from him in the future.

He said, "I want to give it to Shitaa, and I want her to receive it herself."

My aunt answered him with a roughness that my brother did not expect: "She has gone."

After a long time, the truth was known; Shitaa had journeyed to a faraway country, which, after another while, was announced to be America. An immigrant relative had come after a thirty-year absence to see his family and relatives, and he had been surprised by his young cousin, the like of whose beauty and brilliance he had never seen before, neither in the old world nor the new. He had no children by his American wife, whom he was certain would be charmed by Shitaa as well, so he had said loudly in surprise and happiness: "I want her to be my daughter. I will give her the chance to get an education and fortune."

Then he added, as my aunt declared years later: "Here you can't appreciate a great treasure like Shitaa. You usually waste your riches. God only knows what will be the future for such a girl."

My aunt's disabled husband, who was not sorry that his daughter was leaving, said: "Shitaa will find someone who appreciates the jewel that she is. As my wife's uncle has said, 'With our own hands, we kill the most beautiful things we have.'"

My brother became bored waiting for Shitaa to return. After his graduation from the university, he married a widowed relative, whose husband had left her a house and a shop, and he worked in the shop after failing to find a job. Meanwhile, I continued to think about Shitaa, from whom we heard nothing, even after the death of her parents. Sometimes, I would dream that I would see her in an American film or TV series, working as a doctor or a celebrated singer, or else as the wife of a businessman nominated for a political position; I never got bored with looking carefully at the screen, until finally I became addicted to television, but I never saw a woman appearing in an American program with beauty surpassing Shitaa's. My obsession with my absent cousin still grips me, but no one knows the secret I have hidden in the depths of my heart all these years, a secret kept as carefully as I would protect and cherish a precious gem.

My Brother Omar

1

The historic Caliph Omar bin al Khattab entered the life of our family suddenly. He rushed in with a strength we had not expected, as if he wanted to occupy every inch of the house, which had grown too small for its people. Father had always been fond of the biographies of prophets, their companions, and other reformers in the world, and he kept reminding us of them. He would tell us about their lives in the evenings, on religious holidays and national occasions, or during the various crises, such as the disappearance of wheat from the market, the scarcity of coal and gas, or the death of a freedom fighter who was resisting the occupation.

However, in the days preceding the biggest crisis of all, my father began to limit his talks to a few whose biographies filled our consciousness and ears; soon he started talking only about Omar, until we thought (I was little then, no more than eight years old) that Omar bin al Khattab was one of our grandparents, that he had just come back from a long trip, and that he would soon share with us the few beds where our bodies piled together, too many for the quilts to cover everyone or the pillows to fit the many heads competing for them.

In spite of our small house, roofed with wooden beams some of which were buckling, and in spite of the difficulties of living during the World War then, my mother was pregnant for the tenth time. Her belly was swollen from the very first months so that my father's face beamed with joy and he shouted that the coming child would be a male. At home there were already seven children, mostly males, running, shouting, eating with a great appetite, and unwillingly listening to the news on the radio out of respect for their father's concern, which was increasing with the ferocity of the war. He disdained the commands of the French Mandate, which forbade listening to news unfavorable to it. Foreign soldiers had

49

confiscated the few radios in the city, but my father had managed to hide his radio behind the sofa, a radio which he had inherited from his father, its back ornamented with beautiful mother of pearl.

He would sit up straight and announce with determination and sorrow hiding in the premature wrinkles of his forehead (he was not yet 50 years old): "The name of the coming child will be Omar, God willing."

Mother agreed with him and smiled contentedly, a smile that she kept up even on the most difficult days. She moved about the house with her full belly, and we children, boys and girls, would whisper to each other. We had learned how to speak mockingly, thanks to our father's aunt, the spinster who occupied a fixed corner in our living room where she stung people with her looks and comments. And we used to say: "Mother carries Justice[1] in her belly." Aunt, who bore the marks of the Habbet Asseneh disease on her right cheek, would say, "How on earth could justice be carried in a belly or a thigh...!"

2

My father, whose kindly face charmed me, served as chief of the Office of Canonical Courts for many years. Every day he brought home a new story of the cases he had heard in the halls of the court. These remained awe-inspiring in our minds until much later when I grew up and saw the ruins of the court and the wide street running through its yard; I realized then how much my father loved his job and how he had bestowed upon it an eminence that it did not have.

In winter, the family discussions took place around the warmth of the brazier and during the summer days under the trellis on the roof of the house. For my father, these evening sessions with my mother, along with his hubble-bubble, were his times of joy, incomparable to anything else in the world. We heard stories of marriage, divorce, heritage, a quarrelsome second wife who vexed the heart of the children's mother, an eldest son who stole his little brother's

---

[1] Omar bin al Khattab is known for his genius at Islamic law.

heritage, a rich brother who got his poor brother's wife divorced and then married her, adding her to the wives he already had.

Every day there was a new story, and my father would announce sadly, as if witnessing the tragedy itself: "Injustice... injustice. The world is unjust. Woman is poor."

My mother was proud of him, looking at him with a love that can only be compared to her tenderness towards us at bedtime, covering us with that tenderness, passing her rough hand over our heads as she recited from the Qur'an. The caustic soda which she used to wash our clothes had robbed her hand of its softness, but we felt that her palm was softer than silk.

Omar was growing with us since we used to run our hands over Mother's belly to feel his early movements, but my father, in case he caught one of us spying on our new brother, would call: "Do not be cruel to Omar."

However, none of us felt jealous; we had become attached to the coming person as if he were a matchless being.

3

One day, Aunt shouted at us: "Your father is not himself, he eats so little and he rarely smiles."

Resuming her glorification of God in short sentences, which no one understood, she then said: "Have mercy on the man, kids. It's not fair that he be tortured."

Mother was the first to know about the sadness in which my father was drowning, so she would repeat, secretly and openly, either in front of him or in his absence: "Patience...patience."
He would call with agony: "Justice...justice."

We learned that our father was in danger after a judge at the court defamed him. My father's vast knowledge of jurisprudence and Islamic law had upset this judge, so he defamed my father with the French authorities, saying that my father sympathized with the rebels, who had become stronger in the mountains, valleys, and distant neighborhoods. Father had been summoned to the Investigation Department in the basement of the high barracks, and he walked in there self-composed. Although they interrogated him in a dark narrow room where his eyes were blinded by the interrogation lamp, he was let out hours later after having signed a pledge both in Arabic and French that he had no relation to any of the revolutionaries who opposed the regime of the high commissioner. After a while, with great timidity, my mother asked him: "Are you really one of the revolutionaries?"

He looked at her with a severe look that seemed charged with electricity, and so my mother shivered, never having experienced such cruelty from her tender husband. She remained silent for a long time thereafter.

My father never drank alcohol, but he seemed to sway as if from drunkenness, so that he didn't know his way to either the kitchen or the roof, where we had held tranquil gatherings in the old days. At that time my aunt, who was horrified, something that we never expected from her, said: "What would happen to us if the man was fired?"

The bubbling of the water pipe began to sound like moaning, part of the rhythm of everyday events at home where dim silence prevailed, and all us children stopped rushing about; we began talking to each other in whispers. We moved our hands carefully and lightly over the dinner table; there was no more snatching the food joyfully as we had done before. Whenever my father looked at my mother's belly, which was exceptionally big considering that she was still only in her sixth month, he would seem relaxed for a few moments and would call on us, his teeth biting strongly on his ivory lip: "He is coming, no doubt. Omar is coming."

My mother would share with him in his exultation, which she missed; joy showed on her face for a moment like that of a woman promising her husband his first child, but soon she would be perplexed, as his gloominess and distress returned.

When my father stuck his ear to the fabric of the radio speaker, listening to the forbidden radio reports, his eyes glowed when he heard that France was losing the war. He would murmur with a rattling voice, which we understood after we got used to hearing it: "Those who treat others unjustly will be treated the same. Justice is coming!"

One day he came back from work early and sat down next to his aunt, stretching his legs onto the straw pillow to which she resorted to ease the pain of her rheumatic legs. Fear marked my mother's face when she tried to ask him the question.

He said, "I will always be with you at home. I won't be absent anymore."

Mother gasped: "Did they really fire you?"

He nodded with resignation, murmuring, "It was a quick revenge. I should've known from the very beginning that I would surely be dismissed."

4

One night, my mother developed a severe pain in her jaw. Bullets flashed through the sky of the city, horror prevailed in our house, and nothing could be heard but the intermittent moaning of the neighborhood poor in the face of the ricochet sound of bullets. My mother laid her hand on her jaw, which was swollen from an infected molar. She had endured the pain for several days without complaining, but now my aunt's prescription, consisting of anise and cinnamon, had failed to ease it. Her jaw had swollen just like dough when it rises. My father read over it some of the short verses of the Qur'an, passing his hand like a magician over her painful molar. She surrendered to him like a meek, believing child.

Yet the pain did not obey my father's supplicating murmurs. Dawn came with tears flowing from those eyes that used to show only tenderness, and my father, who could not sleep, moved about the house like a prisoner given an arbitrary sentence, reiterating: "Injustice to both soul and body...this is enough, Lord."

When my mother came back from the dentist's clinic, my father was reciting the poetry verses of his dentist friend, the man who had eased my mother's pain with an anesthetic injection. The dentist had recited his own poetry to my father, who learned it by heart and started reciting it again and again to show gratitude for the doctor's efforts to relieve my mother from her pain. That day, Father looked at us as if he had forgotten the injustice done to him at work, and he was replacing many of his sayings about injustice with poetry verses about love. It was as if Omar bin al Khattab had accomplished his historic mission to restore justice in our family life, and we imagined that peace prevailed at home again. For the first time, my father talked about the friendly intervention of a prominent figure in the Al Kutla al Wataniya political party, who promised to restore my father to his job.

My aunt commented sarcastically: "Why? Has the day of judgment come?"

I hated that pessimism in her, and we ignored her dark comment. But what happened in the evening changed the situation and turned our hopes upside down. My mother collapsed while she was sorting the lentils, which had become our inevitable daily meal in spite of the children's protests.

A pool of blood spilled out and froze on the kitchen flagstones, filling the cracks and small holes; the infant, two months premature, was put in the copper washbasin. My mother was laid on her bed, pale; the midwife stood at her feet rubbing them, while Father stood upright at her head reading to her in a low voice, which blended with her whispers calling for help.

What is a miscarriage? We understood about it later, but for Omar to have come into the world lifeless—I could not understand that at the time. Aunt said: "The dentist's anesthetic was the killer."

My father responded, crying, "Injustice is the killer."

Then he commented for the last time: "We waited for him a long time, he arrived dead."

Days and years have passed. I discover that all my brothers and sisters, now spread all over the world with ever growing families, have each named one of their children "Omar." And I, caught up in the hubbub of life, did not have the chance to build a family. But I always said to myself: "If I get married and have a son, his name will be Omar."

I remember how I peeped at the face of my brother, whose tiny body filled the copper wash basin, and I feel profound sorrow that such a beautiful boy was not destined to live.

Part Two

Part Two

Collapse

My father said: "He who has no house has no country." He was a meek seventy-year-old man, and for many years he had been trying desperately to convince me to buy a house, even if one with only a single room, since my circumstances would not allow me to buy a decent one.

He told me, "I won't be pleased with you, son, unless you get a house, one of your very own."

He repeated his threat over and over, even though he himself did not have a house, nor had his father before him. Then he would resume praying with his beads, glorifying God in the corner of the room, which he had never left since the June War. On that subject, he had only once expressed his personal opinion and never added further comment: "The war's not a loss, son, it's a test."

I always would say to him, "One room isn't enough for three people."

Once, when he heard me, he got angry, though gently, and said, "I forbid you to talk like that, son." Afterward, with difficulty he stood up to light an Indian incense stick, which he never used except for the prayers held on the 15th of the month of Sha'ban and on the day of celebrating the holy birthday of the Prophet Muhammad.

"In my dreams I saw that Allah gave you money," he said. "Don't waste it, son. You've got a project here in the country, so invest Allah's money in it."

Personally, I love my father more than any other person, for in addition to his goodness, he thinks clearly and with insight. When I participated secretly in the protests, which shook the city, he said, "Your days are black...but they are teaching you to hope."

And I also loved my wife, who had worked as lightly as a butterfly on the central switchboard of the Provisions Department, where my office faced hers. I adored her angelic voice. In her

57

"Hello, this is Provisions," I seemed to hear the same rhythmically harmonious poetry that I could sometimes hear in emotional songs and other times in poems about country and freedom. Eventually, I became obsessed, during the month of preliminary flirting and then more serious flirting, in listening with all my heart to her voice. This would be possible either through the telephone receiver, when I would make up a need to call her for no purpose other than to hear her voice, or else through the office door, which I left open so that her sweet voice would reach my ears.

When I became crazy about her, I proposed to her on the telephone, but she did not utter a word. I thought she had declined my proposal, so I hurried to her like a child whose toy has been stolen, and I shouted: "Don't you know that I love you?"

And I heard her murmuring shyly, "Me, too," a phrase that made my heart fall happily into her arms.

In the beginning, we spent all our time looking for a place to live, something that made us so tired that by afternoon we could not even exchange passionate kisses. The feeling of exhaustion even limited the words of love that filled my heart

Then, one of her relatives, who was an important dealer in the canned goods business, granted us a favor. He rented us a house, but stipulated we would have to leave the house after two years, because his son, who was studying medicine, would be opening a clinic in it. I gave the relative my word of honor. But when we learned that the doctor had immigrated to Canada to avoid military service, I secretly decided to break my promise and stay in the house despite the owner's requests to hand it over. We had our first child and stayed in the nest that witnessed his birth, his continuous cries as a newborn, his ceaseless noise, his learning to creep, and then his first steps, as if he were trying to get to understand the geography of the house. Yet my father kept saying, "You won't feel happiness, son, until you have your own house."

However, from the first days, when the sweetness of love was still mild and delicious, I had said to my wife, "Listen, honey, take this word from me, attach it as an earring: I hate property, especially private property, so don't try to tell me, 'Let's buy a house, honey.'"

She nodded contentedly. However, when she heard my father talking—she had always liked my father because he never attempted to interfere in the affairs of her kingdom, which she had built and decorated with her own handicraft—about a house we should buy, she shouted cheerfully, "Uncle is farsighted."

We were chatting on our narrow balcony, which overlooked the last tree in the back street; all the other trees had been destroyed by the dust of the building which was being built. "I can't depreciate any of my father's opinions, my dear. As you know he is the wisest of people and the most beloved of my heart, and I am the most beloved of his. But shouldn't we think a little over this decision about a house, seeing as how we have not one piaster to put it into action?"

She jumped for joy, saying, "I knew you would agree."

My father was saying one bead after the other on his amber rosary, which he had inherited from my grandfather, who, it was said, was famous for it in the quarter. It had been the rosary that had given him later, just before his death, his nickname "Kahraman."[1] This became our family name, after our original name, Al-Faqir, was dropped from civil registers for a reason still unknown to me. Al-Faqir (The Poor) is not a name to inspire confidence, so we defended our new family name very zealously. Although some of the old members of the quarter still used the old name, I tried to get rid of it.

Father continued to say his beads monotonously, until he announced one day, "Son, one piaster after another will make the price of the house."

My wife did not need to wait for such an announcement. She started immediately organizing her long campaign of frugality. She kept tight control over our monthly expenditures and showed her ingenuity at economizing all aspects of our life except for the toys of our adored baby. My daily pack of cigarettes became a weekly pack, combined with some licorice candy that she would put in my pocket while kissing me tenderly and whispering: "It might keep your mouth busy, so you can quit smoking."

---

[1] The name of a precious stone.

I was stopped from buying newspapers and magazines, which I enjoyed reading in the evenings. Then, I met a man fond of crossword puzzles, who would buy all the Arabic periodicals. I helped him find answers for difficult puzzles, and, in return, he lent me the papers and magazines. Whenever I filled in a missing letter or provided him a word he could not guess, he would tell me: "You're really an intellectual and a politician."

Because I was fond of history, I knew a lot about Robespierre in the French Revolution and Abi Dhar al Ghifari on Islamic history. I knew about the Protocols of Zion's Wise Men, and the Masonic Movement with its famous people who became leaders and officials in many countries, and I even learned some details about peasants' revolutions in Latin American countries, where the political parties were persecuted because they believed in the rights of workers and poor people. I found out other kinds of information, which I thought at first was merely interesting but which eventually became one of my obsessions.

In addition, we cut down on meat and other proteins in our kitchen as well as our consumption of fruit. We were careful of electricity, lighting only a single lamp after it became quite dark. I tried to think of the lottery, but I remembered the anger of my father, who would repeat again and again his famous saying: "Houses are just like countries, son, they can't be built with money you haven't earned yourself."

I found a second job at night, which meant I doubled my monthly income, but I kept it secret. God can testify I hid it from my father, and my wife helped me do that, for he would never have accepted under any circumstances that his only son among six girls, five of whom were married while the oldest remained single to take care of him, would work as an accountant in a restaurant where wine was served. Until today, my father believes that I was teaching Arabic to a foreign family. He would brag about me, saying, "Didn't I tell you that sound religious education makes a person excel at his language? My son is a living example of that, for he holds a scientific certificate, yet he is so good in Arabic he can teach it to others."

Our bank account grew to the point that we got in touch with real estate agencies. One lead us to a neighborhood far from the city center where we worked, but where the houses were closer to our lifetime goal. My father exclaimed joyfully, his tears pouring from his eyes in wave after wave: "Didn't I tell you, son, hard work pays off!"

He was the first to come with us to the building we chose. It was small, but large in our eyes. We paid half its price in cash, and we were promised early access. I remember that Father murmured on that day, while he was entering the building leaning on his crutch: "Why do they make entrances so narrow? This is not even wide enough for a coffin. Don't they take dead people into consideration?"

But he didn't want to upset us, so he added: "Don't you worry about the entrance, as long as your hearts are big."

And so we had a kingdom extending between the sky and the terrace, guarded by six chimneys, which my wife decided to paint herself whenever they blackened. When we moved in, not much of our furniture was left after we sold the TV and the furnishings for the guest room to pay the balance of the cost of the house. My father insisted on going up to the roof, though his face turned pale from exhaustion. I worried as I helped him up the stairs, and he fixed an amulet above the door, murmuring more than once: "God protect you from evil eye." I wished I could read what he had written on that paper, which he wrapped with thick fabric, then soaked in water, and over which he read seven times the Surat Mariam Chapter from the Qur'an.

That wish of mine stayed with me all the time before the horrifying accident took place, an event that will forever stand between my curiosity and what was written on the amulet.

Everything fell, like salt dissolved in water. The building collapsed in one day. Nothing was left but piles of dirt mixed with pieces of fragile wood and iron rods bent like dry barley sticks. Our kingdom, which had embraced the sky, tumbled down into a hole of sorrow. Everything collapsed...everything.

I remember what happened from the beginning of the dream right down to the painful moment of reality, and I am getting ready to testify in the court, which agreed to hear the lawsuit filed against the contractor by those of us who survived. We were all inhabitants who were outside when the building collapsed. The contractor did not dare to appear in public until the disaster was forgotten. He finally appeared, his head bent over piously, as he told everybody that the experts sided with his testimony. The underground cave on which the building had been built, he said, was responsible for the collapse.

My father, who by this time was unable to speak clearly, murmured: "My son, you are still able to build a new family and a new house."

But I said to myself: "How can I start anything of value without my wife and son?"

The features of my two loved ones were lost in the dirt like two jewels ground into pieces by stones, but I recognized them, even though their flesh had blended with the soil.

The contractor, who was the owner of the building, did pay compensation for the blood of those who died in the building's collapse, according to legal estimations. But I dared not ask him whether he would pledge to rebuild the building with certain materials that would guarantee a solid house that would not collapse because of such irresponsible recklessness. Although the earliest period of grief has passed, I still feel a prisoner of painful memories whenever I see pity in the eyes of others. I also shiver in fear from the new house, as the period during which I must take possession approaches day after day. I do not deny that I am upset when my father talks of this new house, comparing it once more to a country, as if nothing has happened.

For the Sake
of Seven Dollars

1

There's a great deal to say about a small amount of money, over which no sane person could make a fuss, but what happened has happened, and this issue of a trivial amount of money turned into a dangerous matter. The events that took place may be traced far back into history, more than half a century ago, to the day when the man involved was born. Just so, do we conjure up forgotten history, which usually should not be done except in the case of great or influential people.

It seems that the story began on the day when the third son of Salim Istanbulli was born. Salim had just been released from jail after his last theft at the Hal Market. He was broke when he came back to his house, which consisted of two dark rooms in the basement. But he soon became optimistic and announced remorse for his crime after he examined the new baby, born a few days before. It was healthy, unlike the two older brothers, who had been born disfigured and could neither talk nor move afterwards, although the youngest was already seven years old. The newborn proved his superiority over his siblings from the very first day, as he cried a lot, sucked greedily at his mother's breast, and made water whenever he wished, like a prince. Such attributes appealed to the father, who nicknamed his son, proudly and self confidently, the "strong," the "strong fisted," and other such terms.

Salim Istanbulli had always been proud of his kinship to one of the eminent families in Istanbul, the universal capital that had developed into a center of tourism and a destination for those looking for illusory roots. Thus, he announced that his new son, who was registered under the name of Hamid Istanbulli, would become a man of great importance and would correct the orientation of the family, which had been afflicted with bad luck. That luck had pushed him, Salim, to the point where he was accused of borrow-

63

ing money from other peoples' pockets or stealing some clothes
hung out to dry or snatching from the butcher shop a piece of meat
polluted by the breath of a dirty dog.

And so Hamdo al Jack, the name assumed by Hamid Istanbulli
years later, was, before he was one year old, assigned as a sergeant
in the criminal police; that designation resounded splendidly during the great celebration that the father held on his son's birthday,
after he offered the city drug lord a small favor, for which he got a
reward that would tempt him to continue the silent work of drug
trafficking, since he would not be punished for it. Delegations of
well-wishers who approached the baby, still in his swaddling
clothes, put presents under the pillow on which he lay, and repeated as if chanting for the immortality of a leader: "One hundred
years for our sergeant!" The baby cried as if responding to the
greeting in his own language, which had a thousand interpreta-
tions.

Salim Istanbulli's decision to assign his son to the security
forces must have been endorsed by the midwife even before she
heard of it, for she was the one who delivered the new baby with
her hulking hands. Those hands had collected trash for many years
before the woman learned to be a midwife to poor women. She had
learned the skill from a swindling doctor's assistant who married
her to get her gold bracelets but drowned in the sewers before he
could achieve his goal. It was this same midwife who shouted out
that the child would be an important governor one day, and so the
father looked for her afterwards to reward her for her farsighted-
ness by giving her a piece of paper currency of which he was proud
because he had got it, with his own clever fingers, from the jacket
pocket of a merchant who always bragged he had never lost a piaster in his life. The midwife was happy with the reward and added
that the child would be famous when he became a man—as if this
woman, who was never stingy with praise for any healthy baby,
was telling the truth this time.

Hamid's childish ways of acting were a satisfactory expression
of his father's wishes for his son's strength and dominance. When
the child would eat pebbles and soil, Istanbulli would shout, "This
is how men are built," and if the boy would bite a dog or choke a

cat, the father would clap, feeling proud of this son of his loins. When the neighbors complained that the child had become destructive, shooting at lamps with stones and uprooting trees planted in the little park at the entrance of the quarter for the convenience of women and old people, Istanbulli shouted, " Have you ever seen a sergeant in the criminal police sorting out his lice under the sun like weak or cowardly people?"

When Hamid stepped into his early adolescence, his manhood sprouted with no previous warning, and he took the milkman's mute daughter, around whose waist he flung his big arms like a pair of pincers. She surrendered to him; unable to do anything but yell like a mute animal, she twisted in pain out in the deserted yard used as a dump. He shouted with joy, "I'm a stallion." As a result, he dominated the young woman for long months, calling her with his cold looks, like a hyena leading its prey to its den to devour it. When the milkman later suspected what was happening, he preferred to leave the quarter with his family rather than confront Istanbulli and his son, and he preserved his honor by ascribing what had happened to fate. When Salim the father, whose teeth had fallen out, discovered his son's masculinity like that of a stud, he took him to a holy man who wrote amulets in sea ink, which is invisible unless written on a rag taken from the remains of the shrine of a *wali*, or friend of God, who has married four women in one night. The amulet, which Hamid strapped beneath his navel, stayed with him to the end and was one of the secrets of his bullish masculinity. The amulet proved truly effective, just as what the gypsy woman told him about his luck and future proved true. She told him he would become one of the richest of the rich, a prediction which she uttered with the warning, her face assuming an angry expression, not to reveal the grace with which he would be endowed, for, she said, an evil eye can kill and an envious person shows no mercy.

The sergeant's name became Hamdo to satisfy the eminent men of the folksy quarters, who hold heroism and names, which are sources of pride, to be holy. He took Al Jack for his surname to please his first boss during the French Mandate, thus acting like a singer before stardom, who assumes the name of the person whom he owes for introducing him into the world of art and singing.

2

And because Salim Istanbulli was keen from the beginning on making his son take after his father, he refrained from small and open thefts out of fear that his prophecy about his son's eminence would not come true; he proclaimed his remorse in public and pretended that he went to the Holy Places to perform the religious duty of pilgrimage. In reality, he traveled only to a remote village where, after stealing some of its chickens, cheese, and honey, he returned to his home, all his sins forgiven.

Hajj Salim kept boasting that this young man whom he had by divine will would be an important official in charge of security forces, assuming the rank of sergeant, which is the highest rank Istanbulli dared to imagine for one of his descendants. But Hamdo al Jack would disappoint his father. Though he would indeed move forward until he became a staff sergeant, the father was never able to enjoy any of his son's achievements. Istanbulli moved to a lower room too small for his body after it was swallowed in the cellar; he lay there in a heap after being inflicted by a malignant tumor in the intestines, forgotten by his family for many days. The sheikh of the mosque pronounced, "No rejoicing at others' misfortunes, but whoever eats of unblessed money will be punished in his stomach." Because of these words, Hamdo al Jack held a grudge against him and never forgot what the sheikh said. Later, the sheikh's son was among those whom Hamdo al Jack harmed by mercilessly fabricating false accusations against him.

The story of the "sergeant" rank which Salim Istanbulli bequeathed to his son is interesting because it seems to be based on a Moroccan sergeant in the French security forces, who interrogated Istanbulli whenever the police caught him. This sergeant tended to obtain his confessions by notorious methods, the simplest of which was the wheel; under this method of interrogation, the robbers of markets and buses would confess in record speed and go to jail without hesitation. Thus had begun a relationship of one-sided admiration. Istanbulli started to dream that a well-built son of his own blood would become as important as that Moroccan sergeant. He would have the capacity to control people's freedom and he would enjoy drawing facts out of their mouths, utilizing a certain ingenuity that eventually was forgotten by the people of the city after the independence.

What is important in the story of Hamdo al Jack's joining the security corps is that the French commander responsible for the security system himself chose that ferocious young man to become a soldier. The annual wrestling contest was held in working-class quarters under his patronage to choose heroes to be honored with government jobs such as firemen or police. Hamdo was medium-sized; but he triumphed in that contest by using tricks and subtle ways of hurting others to deceive his opponents. Despite being smaller, he beat them one after another and won the championship. As a result, he was summoned by the authorities to submit his papers, which were accepted without hesitation; thus he became a member of Security and was assigned to track men who called for either opposition or rebellion, and to report news of any suspicious gatherings hostile to the foreigners' regime in its last days. In other words, Hamdo became a spy and a lucky student of the Moroccan sergeant, who had taught him the rudiments of the art of that profession.

Hours after independence was announced, Security soldier Hamdo al Jack was one of the first of a group of servicemen who discarded their French uniforms and joined the police of the new national government. Here he proved superior to his colleagues, for he offered important information to the new officials, who, satisfied by that information, became convinced of the noble feelings of soldier Hamdo al Jack. This man, no doubt by virtue of intuitive insight, had foreseen that the day of independence would come and had behaved accordingly. He always excelled at such developments, mutating with the evolution of politics in the country. He specialized in adaptation and flexibility, but a moment would finally come when his abilities began to be questioned.

But in those early days, Hamdo al Jack started a new stage in his life, gradually advancing in the police until he became the most famous sergeant in Security. As we will see, he was the only one unaffected by a change of political circumstances and situations.

He always managed to get either promoted or rewarded whenever some new regime took over the country.

The fortune teller's prophecy gradually was fulfilled, as Hamdo al Jack discovered an important secret, how to get extra money by making bargains with the relatives of those wanted for or suspected of crimes. He would tell the family the hour when an arrest was planned, thus enabling the suspect to flee and allowing him to take his wages, specified according to the importance of the survivor, just before the arrest. This big break came when he began protecting a notable drug lord. The money increased in return for Hamdo Jack's facilitating the drug lord's moves and travels. With time, Hamdo Jack's payment became a fixed share, which he would take from merchants who usually worked behind the scenes, far away from the people of law. His eventual title Al Hajji, usually reserved for men who had completed the pilgrimage to Mecca, was used by those secret partners to refer to Hamdo in public. The name was a result of a nice play on the two initials of his name, turning Hamdo al Jack—H.J.—into Hajji. In the period just before his arrest, he actually thought of heading to the Holy Places to perform the pilgrimage, a religious duty he felt was due, but in the end he did not go. Rather, in accordance with the local custom of resorting to religion after a certain age, he put on a show of religious conduct.

3

Hamdo al Jack suddenly asked to be retired just a few years before sixty. This was supposedly due to bad health, according to the application which he submitted to the administration, but the truth is that he had gotten into a major dispute with his bosses on how to share the revenue from the taxes imposed on the nightclub owners and their increasing numbers of working artists, foreign and local. The dispute pushed him to opt for safety, a decision that contributed to the growing grudge against him, which had been building step by step all these years.

This last installment in the professional life of Hamdo al Jack interested an aspiring television director. He was looking for a satisfactory ending to the idea of a TV series, based on real life, a series he hoped would inaugurate his career in television. The young director had been appointed to the new national television corporation after returning from studying abroad. He had first spent a whole year thinking about the status quo in art and in his newly independent country. He wondered why he felt so detached from it, and finally realized that he was not looking at the reality surrounding him. So he decided to devote himself to looking for facts, real events.

The young director, Ussama K., first learned of the hero of his project (H.J.) through Sergeant Hamdo al Jack's fourth wife, who had resumed her work as a teacher after her obligatory divorce. She was a beautiful, intelligent, quiet young woman, who had been clever enough to discover a hidden side of her husband's life, and the only one among his ex-wives who came to realize the wealth of Hamdo al Jack.

How did she discover this? She lived with him in an isolated house, which Hamdo al Jack had built outside the borders of the city amidst fields of wild cherry and neglected vines; it seemed like the country house of a family, but not one preoccupied with land and agriculture; and thus a promised paradise, which turned into a prison. The gentle young woman had to clean the many rooms of the house, but whenever she asked for someone to help her, her husband would justify his refusal by saying that he did not want any stranger to spoil his privacy with his beloved by intruding in household affairs. At first the wife was not horrified to learn that she might have married a sterile man (she did not hear until later that he had had children by his ex-wives). What really did horrify her was what she discovered in the cellar of the house, a kingdom closed to everyone but him.

Just by accident one day the young wife discovered a path to the cellar, and she followed it out of boredom and curiosity. Through either neglect or forgetfulness, Hamdo al Jack had left the cellar door open. And there was the surprise. Boxes full of gold, silver, drawers stacked with hard currencies like dollars and marks, and a locker made of rare wood, containing an amazing collection of pearl necklaces and radiant jewels. The desk in the cellar, the drawers of which were easy to open just as the boxes were, contained documents and accounts recording the property of her husband, who had never shown signs of wealth. Estates, trucks, stores that sold only European goods, two tourist hotels, a sauna bath, beach and mountain houses, farmlands producing vegetables in greenhouses, a winery in Cyprus, a shipping steamer, and more. All these appeared to be the property of the husband, who had never once offered any of it to the young bride, who had been tempted at first by his promises that had made her forget the age difference. He had always made her feel that he was working hard to secure a decent living, one which his salary could not provide; that was how he had always justified his absences and his travels. She had learned about the travels because of a dress he had brought her, presenting it with the promise that if he succeeded next time, she would have shoes to go with it. On the day of her visit to the cellar, the young woman discovered that she had been deceived. She dared to tell him to his face what she had discovered, but he merely looked at her calmly and accused her of madness. She asked him to give her a little of his imaginary fortune, which she had seen with her eyes and hands. He hopped in front of her like a naked monkey, pulling at the skin on his belly and crying, "Sickness of body and the worries of people, that's all I have, you crazy!" Then he divorced her.

4

So the life of the ex-first sergeant called Hamdo al Jack became the main subject for the young director, Ussama K., who then discovered that his father had been a political victim of H.J. This sergeant was one who demonstrated such tremendous expertise in interrogating accused prisoners that they always confessed, unable to bear the physical and psychological pressures that Hamdo al Jack applied. Like Ussama's father, some of those who survived offered the young director accounts of Hamdo al Jack's deeds. From their testimony, the director pieced together a horrible portrait of the hero of his television series, one complete with all events and scenes. So Ussama K. started drafting the script himself without depending on a screenwriter.

The first episode of the prospective television series covered the childhood period, the family history, and an exact description of the poor quarter where the family lived. The scene describing the labor pains of the mother giving birth to baby Hamid was skillfully juxtaposed with the siege against one of the old revolutionaries who, armed only with an old pistol, took shelter in a muddy hut to avoid the heavily armed French squadron. In the script, the moment the rebel's body scatters in space is the moment when Hamid looks out upon the world shouting more loudly than the very cannons.

The second episode continued the childhood of the series' hero and focused on the education that Hamdo al Jack had received in the cave kept by a thief who claimed that he returned to God in repentance, but who, since he had no other work, must have continued to steal secretly. However, that guess was incorrect. The thief, none other than Hamdo's father, Salim Istanbulli, never stopped working as a spy, providing secret information to the French police about the nationalist parties. French Intelligence rewarded him with enough money to cover the expenses of food and housing, and it seems that the Moroccan sergeant, the ideal whom the father wished his son to be like, was his link with Intelligence. Thus yesterday's executioner became today's friend. Istanbulli's values would be realized as he pushed his son towards strength, control, and violence. The father always boasted so much about the physical power of the young man Hamid that he neglected care for his two disabled sons, who died one after the other like two animals that had lost their claws. Their mother followed them to the grave out of sadness. But on the day of the critical wrestling match, which changed Hamdo al Jack's life and resulted in the breaking of one opponent's arm and the dislocating of another's jaw, Istanbulli was not lucky enough to enjoy his boy's big success. He lay writhing in pain in a dark basement, where he died.

The third episode was dedicated to the French period of Hamdo al Jack's life. This sequence focused on his success acquiring his bosses' trust and marrying his first wife, a woman thirty years old, ten or more years his senior. This wife was the widow of a colonel who seemed to have withered away and died out of frustration because he could not be a stallion and keep pace with her lustful desires, which never slowed down throughout her life. Lust was why she chose Hamdo al Jack, that stocky man with his broad nose and endless energy for loving women. She taught him how to improve his income in different ways. And so Hamdo al Jack's talent for meticulously building a fortune started to bloom. Though he did not speak French well, he always communicated with his wife by body language, which she understood perfectly. Strict as he had been in dealing with the enemies of the Mandate, clever as he had been in collecting rewards and the taxes he imposed on people to protect them, he did not give his wife a farewell look when she left with the army heading back to her home in France. He was ready to begin a new period in his life.

The fourth episode of the series was dedicated to the period after the independence and traced details in Hamdo al Jack 's career in Security as step by step he climbed the stairs after each political change. After one military coup d'etat followed another in close succession, Hamdo al Jack's big nose enabled him to sniff each coming change, so he always came in first. When he asked for the hand of a widow whose husband had been devoured by hyenas during a hunting trip to the wilderness, no one in the family objected to Hamdo's proposal, neither on the basis of his physical appearance nor on the basis of his origins, because, as important real estate brokers, they were betting on him to protect them against the changes in government. However, he deserted that wife after her family lost its property under the Agricultural Reform Law, which nationalized privately owned land. His wife pleaded for and received a divorce, waiving all her rights. As his secret fortune had increased, he wanted to be attached to a family with a good background, but there didn't seem to be enough time for him. For he wanted to keep abreast of the events, always hoping for more booty by which the fortuneteller's prophecy would come true.

The fifth episode of the series focused on Hamdo al Jack's schemes to enlarge his fortune. His third wife was a girl from a poor neighborhood next to his old quarter, as if he felt guilty when his conscience awakened regarding his origins. He took this girl to his house on the outskirts of the city. She was a slow-moving woman who liked sleeping and taking care of her kinfolk. They came to the house in large groups either to eat or to enjoy the color television, the like of which they had never seen in their quarters, where electricity was not yet known. Hamdo al Jack sensed the danger of that large number of people coming often to his little castle and the risk of their discovering the cellar where he hid his secrets. So he divorced his wife without making her angry with him. For the next several years, he worked full time, organizing his commercial and bank affairs in and outside the country; it was a daily joy for him to spend the night calculating and reviewing his fortune in money, property, buildings, and projects. The man was not a miser; rather he was keen on working toward the realization of the fortuneteller's prophecy by hiding his wealth from the eyes of people who know nothing but envy. In spite of his cruelty toward those accused of or wanted for charges ranging from working in politics to breaking common laws, he became less harsh than in the beginning. Actually, he became a model and inspiration to recruits joining the security forces, and his knowledge of interrogation and torture became the object of admiration for the youth being prepared to maintain justice and order.

An important development occurs in Hamdo al Jack's life in the sixth episode. He is alone now and he suffers and hopes to climb to a higher social position. This was something he could never achieve except through political work. So he approaches powerful politicians. But most of them will not forget that he is only a first sergeant in Intelligence and that he was created to serve them, not to be equal with them. He sits alone at home thinking and finds no consolation except with passing prostitutes and mistresses, drowning his sadness in their arms. Being lonely is hard, and when he recalls the barren past, he really wishes Salim Istanbulli had lived to see with his own eye his dreams coming true through his son. But Hamdo al Jack doesn't know despair, so, seemingly under control, he decides to start life over no matter the cost.

In the seventh and last episode based on Hamdo al Jack's life, he looks for a woman's love. Chance leads him to that beautiful teacher who was poor and lonely and who loved his need for a companion to give him happiness. He tempts her with travels and a happy life, and she accepts him. But the new life will not be as completely happy as he desires, for he does not fulfill his promises to her because he is busy with new investments that are available to him with new circumstances. She uncovers his lie and his hidden fortune; they break up. It seems that he had been disputing with his bosses over some illegal booty, which he usually shares with them. This he did in order to dedicate himself to the beautiful, young wife and to start enjoying the fortune, which had not brought him pleasure yet. Things do not go as he wished, for Hamdo is finally caught in the act of trading hard currency after the government announced a fierce campaign to save the country's economy, which was threatened with collapse. The seven dollars found in his wallet raise questions, and Hamdo al Jack is sentenced to a whole year in jail.

5

It should be mentioned that the Television Administration had reservations about the series when it was first submitted. Later, officials admitted that such a work was unlikely to be produced, since it revealed only evil and bad actions; the viewers, they said, would find no glimpse of goodness or honor. The director, Ussama al Kaf, was bitterly disappointed after spending such a long time investigating the reality and writing the script. In the end, he was surprised because the interrogation committee, which looked into Hamdo al Jack's violation of common laws, did not investigate his history and the legendary fortune. The seven dollars in his possession were enough for the committee to set his punishment. The young director decided to retire from his career as an artist, that career in which he had not yet begun to accomplish any of his dreams.

Most probably he did not really retire because of this sentence of Hamdo al Jack's, but decided to take another job which would spare him from surprises and enable him to earn a living no matter what changes might take place in governments or in the affairs of ordinary people.

O Waiting

It was a strange dream, opening up the crowding darkness in my room. The walls collapsed momentarily, and revealed an open space with dark green grass. This became a stage, and as firm footsteps approached me, I was half panicked, half amazed. I heard a deep sound in my ear: "Listen, my son…listen, my son."

My father died many years ago, and memories since that time have piled up in my chest, but he has appeared in my dreams only once, calling me with his beautiful weakness: "Beware, my son, never go to bed feeling sad."

Years ago while we were burying him in a small, silent ceremony, people said that the heart attack that killed him came on after an inspector who was new to the administration accused my father of being a slacker. My father got angry, began to grieve, and died at night in his sleep. My mother said it was the fried eggplants we had received from her brother-in-law's wife, whom she hated, that killed him. At that time I was still looking for an explanation for the death. I was looking for something with which to fill the terrifying void, which overwhelmed me after he was gone.

In the dream, the sentence, which vibrated in my ears, was not exactly that of my father, whose voice I have never forgotten in spite of the years since his death. The phrase, "Listen, my son" sounded coarse, but it captivated me. I felt as if I were walking forward towards that face, which came toward me until it became so close that I felt my face touch his face. His features were not clear, but his upright posture, like that of an aging walnut tree, frightened me; but the sight of the walnuts somehow promised me tranquility and the dream seemed to become a reality. My roof became as high as a distant wall, which split very far away, allowing a venerable old man to enter. His figure radiated with light, and I went toward him as a drowned man who does not fear diving. We met, and I heard him say: "Here I am, my son, listening to you."

I felt as if my tongue had swollen and filled my mouth, block-
ing any words or moans from coming out. I was still trembling with
fright.

My fear was odd, in that it hindered me from filling the house
with screams. I was standing behind my mother, who was prod-
ding my father to wake up but getting no response. She started
clicking her tongue. Full of panic, she said, "He's dead." At first, I
said to myself, "He can't die."

Then I muttered, embracing his body that seemed to me then
still warm, "Could my father die?"

I called to him in his ears while he was still lying on his right
side as usual: "Do you hear me? I'm your son."

The fear I felt then, at his death, struck me again during the
dream that night, as I listened to the figure who had appeared, re-
awakening my old loss. In the darkness, I could not see his mouth
but I heard him say, "Speak, but don't expect that all your dreams
will be realized at once."

Usually, I was full of wishes, but something in me had dulled,
so I could not remember a single wish or specific dream. I was face
to face with the impossible. The figure's speech broke up and
caused me to tremble. He said: "Come on, my son, you have one
chance."

My father always used to say that nothing could alter what
was destined. I believed him, and so my dreams were born of one
another and multiplied during the night; even by day I could not
escape them. Through dreams I was trying to erase what was destined for me, and I knew that at least one dream out of ten must
come true. I did not waste much time dreaming of the impossible.
Although I had inherited many things from my father—such as
reliability, poverty, a government job, and love of work—my
dreams had no link with either my heritage or my habits. They
belonged to me alone; the family had dispersed. No one remained
at home except my mother, who often prayed that I would be lucky
and find a good wife. She prayed for my little sister that she would
have children so that her husband would not divorce her. She
prayed for my elder sister's heart disease to be healed, and she
prayed that my third sister and her husband would come back

home after their long absence in distant countries, where the heat is severe both winter and summer.

The night was at its end, and I had not slept much after sympathizing with my mother's sighs during her sleep. Those sighs increased night after night as her rheumatism became fiercer, and I kept tossing and turning in my bed like someone in a fever. I thought about that sad woman in my office whose charm was increased by distress; her black dress was the black of night, in which I envisioned a sea to drown my longing for her. But I met nothing except rejection.

This sad woman had begun to work in my office, and the under-ministry had celebrated her, as it never had a new employee. Her coming was veiled in obscurity from the first day, for the news of her husband's assassination had reached us before she had, and her face wore a tragic smile that added to her charm. One day I told my mother about the widow and her children, whom she was raising, and my mother looked at me with eyes full of tears from peeling onions and said: "A woman never forgets her man."

Secretly, I did not believe her, for I had begun to hope that the widow might be a willing mate. Her attraction to me seemed to me to exclude others. My insomnia lasted for a long time that night before my resistance weakened and I drowned in a floating sleep, only to hear his voice urging me to wake up.

The old man said again: "Come on, my son, a new chance is ahead of you."

"One chance? For one wish?" I spoke in a low voice, but the old man guessed my words and said: "You have now the chance of one dream which I can realize for you." Then he added, inspiring my hopes: "So choose your dream."

Fog and mist came in and woke me, and I could not see the old man anymore. The glow that encircled him like a colorless dress disappeared, my elation turned to fear, and the belief I sought was attacked by disbelief.

I spent the rest of the night trying to tell myself that nothing had happened. In spite of my uninterrupted series of dreams, I still believed firmly that physical reality is undeniable and dreams are false. But the old man's face stayed in my mind. Wrapped with captivating ambiguity, this image seemed to confirm the reality of what happened to me. I told myself that even if the phantom of the old man was an illusion, the promise was real. I had heard his words, and they still remained with me, clearer than a prayer in a silent holy dawn. I hesitated to tell my mother about my dream visitor during morning coffee, her regular habit with my father, but she interrupted my silence and without looking at me said: "Don't stay up at night a lot...your health can't stand it."

Then, groping for the absent Arabian jasmine on her breast, which had remained unadorned after the departure of her husband, she said: "I saw your deceased father in my dreams, and he said good fortune will enter our house." She looked at me tenderly and continued: "He meant for you, son."

I realized then that the house had received two visitors on one night and decided to take the old man's promise seriously. Thus I went out to a new day.

I hoped the widow would be the first person I encountered in order to stimulate, from the sadness of her face, a longing that would lead me to the warmth of her body, wrapped by the black dress and contained by deprivation. But my wish was in vain, for instead, the early employees and their conversations about high prices (one of them calling confidently, "It is one of the signs of war,") confronted me suddenly.

I said to myself: "Shall I ask the old man of promises to make life easy for us, us whose small incomes can not fulfill legitimate hopes?"

When the sad woman entered, I rejoiced and renewed my hope, thinking, "Will my only wish be union with this wonderful woman?"

They called her "Um Sakhr," that is, the mother of Sakhr, and I was the only one who called her "Mrs." At first, she looked at me apprehensively. But after a few days, she sensed my boundless respect for her tragedy. So she accepted my carefully calculated approach to her. Nevertheless, she could not have understood the secret fire flaring inside me as I dreamed of her emerging white from her blackness, just as life emerges from death.

I stepped aside from her a bit, away from the others, who continued talking about the difficulties that face us daily. "Are your kids all right?" I said.

She appeared to be listening to the other conversation, nodding like someone resigned to a necessary acceptance. She turned and replied, "The kids are all right."

Trying to assume a courageous attitude, I gathered all my strength and asked her: "And are you...all right?"

She gave me an absent-minded look but did not answer a word.

Well, here we are, I thought. I am older than thirty and so is she. But tragedy had erupted in her ripe body, giving her the vitality of a virgin close to twenty, while early old age was creeping into my limbs like monstrous ants.

I said to myself: "If only I could ask the old man to keep me far from senility and disability as long as I live."

I said to her more boldly after she accepted my invitation for morning coffee, something she had never done before, "The past is gone. The living deserves our attention more than the dead."

She froze in place as if a thunderbolt had struck her castle of secrets, her eyes turning red out of anger. She soon got hold of herself and stared at me in a way she had never done before. I shivered and got goose bumps. I did not know what to do with my sudden shyness, the shyness of a teenager. The only way before me was to invent a question: "Who takes care of the children while you are away?"

She answered coldly: "I can depend on my two boys' early manhood."

Words rushed into my mouth in sudden audacity: "I'd like to get to know them."

Her mouth turned up in a quick smile and she opened it a little but said nothing. I wished I had filled the silence with a crazy kiss. I realized that among the staff I was specially privileged, so I told myself: "I will not ask my father for her. It is certain that I will have her. Let me look for something else to ask the old man for."

It was a day full of yearning for the lady, whenever the chance presented itself, and of thinking, which kept me from work. So I accomplished nothing. I was thinking only of the one wish I would ask for that night in my dreams. "My father would not come back to life again even if I wished that," I said to myself.

So I decided that I would make up my mind concerning a wish that could be realized. A fortune! I thought if I had a fortune it would help a lover like myself build a nest to protect a small family. Then I continued, saying to myself: "How great it would be to have a four-wheel drive car to breeze over the mountain paths. The wet wind will blow as we laugh and sing."

I remembered my father lying down, as he always liked to do while watching television, so he sat up, looking up at me lovingly, and saying: "No matter how harsh the difficulties are, my son, an honest man should hold to his principles and be an altruist."

I never dared to argue with him, even in spite of his subtle manner in discussion. I was not afraid to oppose an opinion of his, but my love for him pushed me to agree with him always, to assume unconsciously an absolute belief in his principles and thoughts. Later, when I sat by myself, I often said: "What benefits have these values brought him?"

Nevertheless, I had never dared to oppose any of his sayings, to the extent that when we were entrusting him to the heart of the earth I thought I saw him emerging from the grave like light, easy and soft, to settle inside me and never leave.

When Um Sakhr was assigned to my office, I did not know that the other offices had rejected her out of fear, and I was the last to know that her husband, who had been involved in politics, was chasing her with his curse even after his death. When the lady settled finally under my supervision, I noticed many men who admired her sad beauty start visiting the room under trivial pretexts. She never showed an interest in anyone. I was hoping that her interest was saved for me, so I was pleased. After a long period of silence one day, I asker her: "How long can mourning last?"

Her sharp looks confused me like nails scratching my face. I realized then that I must have made a mistake, but I did not retreat; instead, I tried to make up for the previous slip of tongue: "That black dress suits you...but..."

She stood erect, carrying papers in her hands, and headed away towards the filing cabinet. I could not bear her sudden rejection of me or the looks of the employees at the other end of the room, which had once been a place for interrogating prisoners. I walked out of the office, covered with an embarrassment that led me as far as the street, where I joined its tumultuous traffic. My breath quickened and I did not calm down until I began thinking of the old man in the dream and my telling him: "I have only one wish, I have no other."

He would say, "Say it, my son, and I will fulfill it for you without hesitation."

My father's voice spoke to me from within, calling, "Do not be extravagant about your wishes."

I answered, seeking refuge: "My wish is never to know either sadness or fear any more."

I felt the old man would look at me with a smile that I had never seen on his face before and he would nod. Then, approaching me, he would probably pat my shoulder with his white hand and go away.

My mother was surprised at my coming back from work unusually early; she raised her eyebrows to express her amazement, but soon she went into the kitchen and let me continue waiting for what was coming.

I repeated to myself: "I do not want to know sadness or fear, that is my wish."

Whenever I recited that wish to myself, I felt the old man standing in front of me, looking at me doubtfully, as if asking me to repeat, so I would. I looked at my watch and found that I still had time before night, so I thought again, but could find nothing other than that wish to ask the old man for.

Darkness came, midnight, dawn, I went back to work. The old man had not appeared. I said to myself that there must have been a misunderstanding. I still wait for the coming of the night, but nobody appears and days pass. Waiting is not fruitful. My mother is diminishing like a tree discarding its leaves. The lady becomes more beautiful in the blackness of her dress. Her pride leading her to rejection of me arouses my grief. Days pass, each the same. From time to time, I ask myself: "It seems that my wish was difficult to realize..."

And so I excel at the game of waiting...

Whatever Happened to Antara[1]

The end of the day had been bad. To lose was one thing, and to live trembling out of fear of punishment was another. I knew my punishment would be harsh after the new, colored shirt was torn; I had borrowed it without permission from my oldest brother's closet, where I discovered pictures of different women carefully stuck on wood. Not one looked like a relative or neighbor girl. But I did not spend time searching for the truth behind those pictures, as any curious person might do if he discovered a secret among old clothes. All the clothes in the closet were old, except for that one new shirt, which, I had been sure, would give my appearance some strength; it also covered my body loosely and gave me comfort and freedom of movement. I imagined I would be the envy of the children in Al Ainain Quarter, those poor ones who eyed even my trousers jealously, let alone that colorful shirt. But things did not go as I expected.

The slap I received on the back my neck was nothing compared to the traces of long fingernails that the fight left on my arm. After coming back victorious from his football match and after learning what had happened, my brother surprised me by saying: "Did you take your revenge on the monster?"

I did not utter a word; instead, with bowed head, I kept staring at the ground to avoid his looks, which appeared explosively angry.

I hid the torn shirt in the bottom of the basket of dirty laundry after I sneaked into the house. I knew my brother wore that shirt only on romantic occasions, the secrets and details of which he hid from everybody. When he learned what had happened to the

---

[1] An Arab hero and poet who is the subject of traditional storytelling. He was a half-black slave who became, because of his prowess and horsemanship, an indispensable warrior of his tribe. Antara is known sometimes as Antar, the name of this story's character.

shirt, he waved his hand in my face, and said: "You coward! You let him rip your arm and you didn't do anything about it?"

Although he seemed very angry, he picked the shirt out of the basket, waved it, and threw it at me haughtily without giving it a pitying glance. He kept staring at me with angry looks and murmuring: "I can't believe it. He knocks you out...and you don't defend yourself!"

In those moments, I felt that I loved him more than ever. Although my brother played the role of a father with his strict rules and his incessant surveillance over my study and behavior, he never denied me money, some of which he earned working as a mechanic. He did this in addition to studying, in order to supplement the family income, which had declined in value because of the increasingly high prices during the war. I swore that I would avenge myself and my brother's colorful shirt.

The battle was not equal, but I emerged with the least damage possible. Antar was fourteen years old, about my age, and his body was composed of no less than seventy kilograms of fat, flesh, and grossness. While his breasts, rounded under the cotton shirt that always stuck to him because of the sweat oozing from his body, made him look as doltish as a young woman flaunting masculine manners, his dark brown complexion gave his reddish eyes a glare that would stir horror in any heart. Antar's smile never seemed to leave him since his mouth was open all the time and he chewed anything he could lay his hands on. This provoked the ire of both young and old, but no one dared to pick a fight with him, so he became the unrivaled master of the quarter, doing whatever he wished. People would steer clear of him to avoid his evil, so if he stretched out his hand to steal a cucumber from the load of a donkey, the owner would respond, "Good health, Antar." Such a surrender never occurred to me, so the battle was on.

I was small, but my lightness helped me to move like a cat, and Antar bellowed like a barbarian out of anger because he could not catch me. For that reason the ones who had nicknamed me "Gul," or marble ball, were proved right. The first people to give me this name were two of my brother's friends who threw me to each other in their sportive arms like the small marble I was fond of playing with. I was the best at shooting it and eventually became a champion of this game in Al Ainain Quarter. So back to the battle. I threw myself in all directions so that Antar could not grab me; Antar's nickname had been imposed on the boys of the nearby quarter too, so people had forgottem his real name. His super strength allowed him to impose his own taxes: he never let a child pass through his kingdom without mugging him, stealing his piasters or candies, whether from hands or pocket or perhaps even from a child's mouth. Antar would pick candy out with his index finger, like an iron pincer stretching into the terrified mouth. When Antar got what he wanted, he would look at it with joy and laugh boisterously like a genie, saying: "From mouth to mouth, the mother dies."

This proverb was common as a spell against infectious disease, always a danger and often out of control at a time when medicine was rare.

When I came back from that battle, my mother looked at my face, checking silently and reproachfully, dressing my wounds with the black ointment that was always available in a house full of children. My grandmother, who had come to live with us after being widowed, used to say that we children split the ground and popped out like genies, My father had welcomed her as part of the family and had stated over and over that she was no burden despite the hardness of life. Listening like a respectful, knowledgeable person to the news broadcast of a forbidden radio station, nodding her head as the announcer commented on the news of the flaming revolution in progress against the French, my grandmother seconded him and murmured: "You'll be victorious, God willing."

Then she would scold me: "What you need is a nurse, not a mother." Later, with the tenderness of a weak person and smiling to my mother, she turned down the radio out of fear of our neighbor, whose collaboration with the French colonialists we heard much about.

She said, "Have mercy on your hard-working father. He can't buy a new shirt every day."

At that, two tears rolled from my eyes, and my mother, overwhelmed with pity for me, cried also.

"How gentle you are, my son," she said, "always thinking of your father's situation."

The reality the day of the battle is that I was suffering from the pain of those hard fingernails, which had scraped my flesh while I had not been able to do likewise to my enemy, Antar.

It had all started when Antar had shouted at me, as I passed along the narrow lane heading towards the earthy hill where children gathered for games of marbles. I had thought my shirt would protect me against the aggression of Antar, whom I had not talked to or faced yet, so I ignored his calls, but then he cried out angrily: "You, boy—the one with the French shirt!"

The insult seemed so direct that I couldn't ignore the matter any more. Blood boiled in my head and my spit fell between his feet. He stood silent for a moment in amazement as if facing a challenge he had never known before. His lower lip hung down, and two of his canine teeth glittered in the strong sunlight; this combined with his idiotic smile destroyed the courage I had shown in my surprising response to his insult, but I pulled myself together against all possibilities and waited for what might happen.

During those moments, I felt as if an enemy tank was moving toward me. Antar walked one step closer, then stopped. Children behind him watched. Their eyes seemed full of pity, or maybe they were rejoicing at what was happening to the new kid in the quarter, or perhaps they found in me courage they never knew they had. I gradually felt more composed until Antar shouted in a steely, horrifying voice: "When Antar commands, he must be obeyed."

My reaction was faster than my thinking, even though the situation needed no explanation, for there was no doubt he was capable of destroying me.

"I'm not afraid of you," I shouted. "You don't scare me."

And after taking a step toward him, I added: "And my shirt is *not* French."

The monster had nothing to say; it was his hand that talked; his heavy palm flew in the air to strike me. I dodged it by stepping backwards, and the battle was on. He was chasing me, and at first, my speed saved me from his talons. I avoided his grip when he tried to get grab me, and each time this happened, his agitation increased. This agitation found an outlet in the bad language pouring from his foaming mouth: "You son of a whore!"

I didn't answer, focusing on how to escape him.

"You imitator of infidels!"

The colorful shirt seemed to be the cause of his rancor, and it did not escape his nails, which finally got me; the blood flowing from my arm put an end to the brutal battle, which was stopped by a turbaned sheikh as he came out of the nearby mosque. He separated us, and grabbing my hand, led me out of the quarter. And I started running with all the strength I had, though my desire for vengeance grew fiercer moment by moment.

The days of that war were tough, but I did not allow myself more of the food mother was economizing on. I figured that if I could gain weight I would win the second round, so I thought of lifting weights to acquire strength. But my brother found out about the exercises I was doing on the roof and stopped me, saying they might stunt my growth. He pressed my shoulder affectionately, and said: "It's okay if you're weaker than your opponent, but you have to be smarter to win."

"How...how...?" I asked.

So my brother whispered as he was leaving for his night job: "Mind is the strongest part of any human being."

Later, I learned that the lad Antar was living with his mom in a room at an old inn; part of the inn had been turned into a stable, the rest was occupied by destitute families taking shelter there, despite the cracked walls. No one knew who Antar's father was, so I began to think that his mother, who worked as a servant in the houses of French officers, had conceived a child by one of those African soldiers who accompanied the officers and were famous for raping women when they were drunk. So I convinced myself that the bad boy Antar was a bastard in whose veins ran the blood of the enemies. I decided I would throw this disgraceful charge in his face once we met again, and see whether others would all band together against him. I said to myself: "I'll see if this savage beast will dare to show his teeth in my face afterwards."

Antar's suspicious origin became a topic to mention whenever I got the chance, at school and in the quarter. But at home, while she was weaving again some wool that had warmed us in the past years, my mother said: "It's a sin, son, to raise doubts about people's lineage or honor."

I answered her boldly, as if Antar's doubtful origin were indisputable: "If you saw the color of his complexion and his beastly behavior, you would agree with me and say he really is a bastard, that his father is undoubtedly a Senegalese," and concluded with determination: "He is our enemy."

My mother repeated her warnings to me and exchanged looks with my grandmother, who listened without offering comment. Then the conversation stopped completely, for my father came in suddenly to announce with unrestrained joy: "Well, at last, the city has started to move. People are gathering everywhere for demonstrations."

My mother instructed us to return home immediately after school, as soon as the chaos started. We were too little to participate in any demonstration against armed soldiers, she said. However, the demonstration set out tempestuously from As-Sultani School. Little kids joined adults and boys from distant quarters, chanting against the French occupation, waving knives and sticks, demanding freedom and independence. At that moment, I completely forgot what it means for a boy to disobey his mother.

The city had almost closed down. The protestors showered stones on those shops that had not responded to the call for a public strike, so glass shattered, signs fell, and the sound of whizzing bullets resounded from behind the bridge. Then, that sound of bullets came from all directions and scattered the demonstrators, who hurried to hide in any entrance of a building or behind any parked car. Some simply fell to the ground on their faces to avoid the bullets the French were firing directly at the people.

Surprise stopped me from running away; I stood unbelieving, watching the evil boy, Antar, leading grown men along, approaching the column of soldiers who were shooting in all directions. Antar himself was advancing, his shirt torn, showing his chest, and he was chanting, "Down...down..."

The crowds of demonstrators retreated, and no one remained except three men, led by Antar. His stick had fallen and his brown chest was dyed with splattered blood, yet he ran like a bull towards a group of black African soldiers whose faces and teeth were glittering under the blaze of the sun. Then he stumbled and fell down on his face; he was one motionless mass on the ground. I sensed danger, so I fell flat on my belly and hid my face in the dirt. During the moments I lay there, I could not decide whether the sorrow which filled my eyes with tears was regret or sadness for that boy Antar, whose chest was ripped open by dum-dum bullets.

This mixed feeling stayed with me a long time; I still don't know how to clarify my feelings. I go to visit the old inn, after many years, as a tourist; curiosity compels me to become acquainted with this place, which had become a shelter for the destitute and for animals. Unfortunately, I could not find anyone among its new inhabitants—whose friend is still poverty—who could recall that fierce lad whose name was Antar. Have people really forgotten him?

As I grow older, I continue to consider my attitudes, and find that I still cannot separate sadness from remorse in many situations, not just in the death and disappearance of Antar.

The Picture of the Naked Man

1

I decided to find the picture that was lost—or hidden somewhere, let me say—for none of my documents or papers could possibly be lost because I usually keep each in its place. I am famous for my scrupulous care of materials, known for my precision, and was once nicknamed "the man of archives." For example, I still keep the first unclear draft of a novel that has been rewritten five times and the preliminary sketch of a story that has been redone twenty times at least. In addition, I collect newspaper clippings recording an accident in which a person I knew at school is involved. Thus I know a lot about the life history of some schoolmates who have become ministers, officials with great responsibilities, famous contractors, merchants, or real estate agents. As for those among them who are not famous, like common workers or the poor, who are ground down by the hardships of life, I hold only sweet memories.

The drawers are full, my closets are crammed with books and papers; not a single empty spot can be found on the walls of my office, so the paintings of which I am proud and which I have bought or had given to me as presents are doomed to pile up in the attic, waiting for space in the house; an army of books and cabinets is creeping slowly toward its walls.

In my office, cabinets stand like a high dam. Their sides form the room where I move in calculated and sometimes annoying freedom. In that beautiful prison, I sometimes get angry enough to yell in that space; sometimes I feel happy for an unknown reason or sad also because of a piece of news I heard about a catastrophe that has hit a country or drowned some people crossing a river. With the passing of time I have developed into a high fidelity receiver.

I knew that I still had the old photograph that had disappeared. I still remember that I wrote a sentence on the back of the photograph, when my friend and I were still senior students at the

91

Tajhiz High School. I started to repeat to myself the sentence as if I had just written it: "The memory of my standing by accident in the back garden of the school next to Samir al Ajeena, whom I expect to be a master at opportunism and a teacher of cheating and deceit."

The story of the photograph actually began in the cafeteria, which puts me together with my morning cup of coffee. I was reading on the local page of the newspaper that my schoolmate Samir al Ajeena was being summoned from his work at the embassy to take a very high position in our country, "which needs the efforts of people like him," they wrote. I thought, "They must have learned about his smuggling hard currency," and from that moment memories surfaced one after another. It was at that point that the idea of looking for that photograph occurred to me. In that photograph, my schoolmate Samir, short and stocky, has laid his arm on my shoulder as if he wanted to contain me. He is smiling in his own way while the shadow from his light moustache turns his smile into a sarcastic look that one could never forget. Samir al Ajeena is back in my mind.

I still remember dear Saami, my closest school friend, using his camera to take that picture of Samir al Ajeena and me, the camera that would become the means of his livelihood in journalism and later would ruin his career due to his insatiable curiosity. He would shoot, with artistry and skill, both the funny and ugly sides of different personalities who worked in economics and politics or had other kinds of prestige. Samir fell down into a sewer hole, people said, and this was very surprising to me as well as to his colleagues. Who could be blamed? Then the idea that he was drunk before he fell into that hole, which the municipal workers had forgotten to cover, spread among the people. But his childless widow did not believe it; she swore that he had never tasted wine during his life with her. But mostly she kept silent and finally disappeared completely from the city.

When I was sure that Samir al Ajeena had returned from his diplomatic work abroad, I hurried to my documents to look for that solitary photo of him and me. I do not remember ever having stared at it with much attention before except for once when I was storing it with the many other photos I had not yet found time to include in my album of school pictures. "I have really neglected tidying up my cabinets," I said to myself as I looked through my drawers and shelves, blaming myself more and more for being careless. Something like a fever spread through me as I failed to find that photo, until something happened that turned all search attempts upside down. My eyes and hands settled on a lower drawer, the edges of which were covered with calcified dust, as if many years had passed since I last opened it. The drawer was filled with papers, dossiers, and notebooks. I thought I heard a faint voice, calling for help as if from a deep well. No one but me was at home. My wife had not returned from work, and the kids were at the neighborhood playground. The radio was silent and the tape recorder still on. But the faint voice went on, and I felt a wave of fear, which started down deep inside and eventually finished as cold sweat that I wiped off my forehead.

The more I looked through the papers and flipped through dossiers and notebooks the closer the voice came, and I even heard my name being mentioned every now and then with that supplicating voice. "Release me...release me..." it called, and as the moments passed, my fear turned into curiosity, mixing with and fighting that fear. "Release me, I do not want to stay a prisoner any more," said the voice, which was clear now as if it were coming from close by or even from a face close to mine. When I got out an old yellow notebook, the voice became suddenly human.

On the cover page of the notebook, I had written "the Project of a Novel," and under that phrase I had written with a pencil, "These papers are to be torn up because they are not good enough for publishing." Twenty-six large-sized pages covered with writing were inside, the main part of an unfinished novel, Soon the voice was squeaking in my ears: "I beg you to put an end to my prison," it cried, and I closed my eyes, surrendering to something which was no longer fear or curiosity.

2

With his plump build he stood before me, naked except for striped shorts, the lines of which magnified his corpulence. He was shivering as if in fear; my eyes, which were circling him as if searching for words for an indecent description, focused on him, so he trembled. Soon he murmured, "You left me like this, naked, twenty years ago."

"Oh! I remember now, I remember you quite well, for I actually left you in a panic in her bedroom; the sudden arrival of her deceived husband meant you had nothing to hide your nudity but these silly shorts."

He answered feebly, "In fact, it was she who seduced me." With barely concealed admiration, he added, "She was charming, no man could resist her beauty."

I stared at him with resentment filling me, filling even my breaths, and I said through my teeth, "You entered the bedroom of a woman like a thief, and who is that woman? The wife of your comrade in political struggle!"

The deceived husband had been assigned an emergency mission outside the city, but he had finished his work quickly. Driven by his longing for the woman's body, he had returned early, and the traitorous friend was trapped. The naked man stood behind a desk as if he wanted to veil his nudity, and he shouted like a mortally-wounded man: "I was going to jump out of the window, but my fear of height stopped me."

I said, "I won't hide any secrets. I was thinking then of letting you fall down and have your bones smashed, but I changed my mind at the last moment."

The trembling man said to me: "I stayed like this, terrified, waiting for the moment when the husband would arrive with a gun in his hand."

Correcting him, I said, "Say the gun which you yourself gave him as a present to defend himself against traitors and enemies."

His head lowered, the naked man said: "Do you really want me to die just for a passing meeting with a woman?"

"Wasn't she a woman worth dying for?" I asked with derision.

He shouted with a sternness embodying his nature: "Nothing is worth dying for."

"What about principles and noble goals?"

He remained silent and resumed begging in the moment of his utmost weakness. At that time I sent my words along with the smoke I was enjoying.

"Rather I wanted you to suffer for reasons other than betraying friends."

I was proud of that decisive sentence. Turning round and taking pleasure in relaxing in the chair, I said: "It is your record, which is full of opportunism, changing loyalties and seeking personal interest, that has pushed me to hate you. Do you remember? I do not think you've forgotten your dramatic maneuvers among parties. At one time you are the religious man, at another you are the socialist combatant who would not compromise over principles. Then you are the fanatic nationalist, but next you are the advocate of internationalism. I should have called you the chameleon, but that poor animal changes its colors to defend its existence when threatened. You did what you did to threaten the existence of others..."

The naked man shouted back, moaning: "Don't you see, we are all doomed to go with the current. It is stronger than our weak personal entities. Isn't human weakness worthy of your mercy?"

3

I had completed twenty-six pages in just one day and one night back in the days of my youth. Filled with indignation, I wrote those pages of the first chapter of a novel that was destined not to come to light. It seems that indignation led to my burying the pages in that old drawer, waiting for a day when my resentment would cool down and I could return to the novel. But days passed quickly as usual, work piled up, new ideas emerged, and there was no place any more for that manuscript among my projects.

The naked man shouted, again.

"And now!"

"What about now?"

"It's time now."

I looked at him, contemplating his anger and fear. Enjoying his misery, I told him: "There is no way out for people like you but to wait."

"Aren't twenty years enough!"

Kneeling down, clasping his hands under his chin to beg, he started hissing with the voice of an old man: "Get me out of this state, and I will be your slave." Then invisible tears mingled with his hissing: "Do whatever you want to me, but put an end to this prison and my deadly stasis."

Then he sat upright like an Indian fakir and began murmuring unintelligible words as if reciting a prayer that no one but himself understood, so I just shrugged indifferently.

In my novel, the hero did not refrain from anything in the way of his goals, even murder, which he thought of but did not dare carry out. He stabbed his friends in their backs, though without blood; he sullied the reputation of his friends with lies, he bowed with the wind wherever it went. Why did I stop writing about him? Well, I feared he would become an example to be followed. But in spite of my deep hatred for him, I had enjoyed writing about him. At first I had imagined that I had been given the task of exposing the truth of this swindler, but the joy of writing pushed me toward details, and I found myself fascinated by the characteristics that revealed his true humanity, that in itself was paradoxical, composed of beauty and ugliness, good and evil. So I stopped, after twenty-six pages.

Coming toward me with firm steps, then more normally, the naked man said, "Look at me. Hasn't your big heart softened? Think of my misery, don't I deserve mercy after this punishment that took such a long time?"

At the time, I had convinced myself to go on. "I must continue the chapters of the novel to the end, for I have become more understanding of the human soul and thus more capable of detecting the place of deficiency in virtue."

Undoubtedly, I felt some sympathy for the naked man, who was now whirling in the room round himself like a dervish, getting closer to me and then farther away from me, wet with perspiration as if he were washing his past in the tears of his body.

"Is it time to forget?" I murmured and followed his whirling; he was looking at the ceiling with no awareness of his surroundings. The scene looked as if the sky were opening up new horizons for him.

"Time for forgiveness."

Printed and bound by CPI Group (UK) Ltd, Croydon, CR0 4YY

13/04/2025